ART OF CUNNING

A STEAMY FOX SHIFTER ROMANCE

STEFFANIE HOLMES

BACCHANALIA HOUSE

Copyright 2015 Steffanie Holmes. Second edition copyright 2017 Steffanie Holmes

ISBN: 978-09951222-9-1

http://steffanieholmes.com

Want free books, exclusive giveaways and exclusive sneak peeks at upcoming Steffanie Holmes paranormal romance books? Sign up for the mailing list to get the scoop.

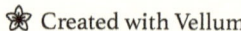 Created with Vellum

1

ALEX

"James Alexandra Kline!"

I cringed as my full name reverberated off the hallway walls. Through the glass wall in my office I could see Matthew storming toward me, his round face puffed up like a pimple about to burst. Across the hall, Tara – the visiting collections curator – looked up from her desk, her face alight with the promise of intrigue.

Matthew was mad. Which meant only one thing. He'd found out that—

"James Alexandra! The Raynard exhibit is opening in two weeks. Where the *fuck* are my paintings?"

I sank down lower behind my desk, wringing my hands in my lap. I'd known this confrontation was coming. In my head, I screamed at him that they weren't "his" paintings. Matthew Callahan was the director of the modern art department at the Halt Institute, a prestigious art gallery in the heart of Crookshollow village. He could no more paint an exquisite work of art than he could recognise one. He didn't even really *care* about art. He had only one trait that made him a competent curator: he was loud and bolshy and could usually get his way. Except, of course, when his assistant curator messed things up.

The assistant curator being me, although judging by Matthew's voice, probably not for much longer.

"Well?" Matthew loomed in my doorway and barked. "Do you have anything to say for yourself, *James*?"

"No," I muttered, staring at my knees. I hated it when Matthew used my real first name. He only did it because he knew it made me uncomfortable, and Matthew loved making people uncomfortable. Silently I cursed my parents for naming me – their only daughter – after James Fauntelroy, my famous male ancestor. *Who does that?*

But now wasn't the time to be thinking about my parents, especially since that usually brought up some tough memories. I had a bigger, angrier problem hurtling through my office door.

A thousand excuses loomed on my lips. It wasn't my fault the paintings were late. The Halt Institute won the contract for one of the most anticipated exhibitions in the entire country. The artist, Ryan Raynard – despite being one of the darlings of the modern art scene (and my favourite English artist) – was a recluse. He lived in his family's crumbling manor not far from my own flat in Crookshollow, but he hadn't been seen outside the manor walls for at least ten years. Despite never having exhibited, never doing press, and never schmoozing with the rich collectors who made the art world go round, Raynard was one of the most sought-after artists painting in the modern impressionist style. Buyers snapped his pieces up as soon as they hit the auction houses. His paintings leached into the market through his secretary, Simon Host, who was the man I had been dealing with over Raynard's first-ever public exhibition.

Everything had gone well initially, until I needed to have the paintings shipped to the Institute. Despite numerous calls, emails, and even a drunken attempt to smoke signal from the pub last night (courtesy of my flatmate Kylie helping me drown my sorrows) to Simon's office, I'd heard not a single reply about the delivery of the paintings.

Of course, Matthew didn't care about any of that. All he saw was a big gap in the warehouse where the Raynard paintings should've been, and a staff photographer getting paid to Instagram pictures of his nostrils.

Matthew leaned against the doorframe and scowled at me. He'd curled the ends of his moustache with wax, so it looked as if he was smiling and frowning at the same time. "Gareth isn't working this weekend. If those paintings aren't here by tomorrow, the photographs don't get shot until next week, which means the advertisements don't get to the printers on time, the *Guardian* holds back our editorial, and I start wondering why on earth I hired someone so goddamn incompetent."

I gritted my teeth. "I know all this, Matthew. Raynard's office is being difficult, but I've got it under control."

"Tomorrow, then. On your head be it." Matthew shot me a final, deadly stare, and continued down the hall to harass another curator.

I rose and shut the door, turning the key in the lock so Matthew couldn't walk in again. Across the hall, Tara – another curator – waved at me through the glass. I glared at her and pulled down the shade, hoping she hadn't noticed my red face and shaking hands.

I slumped back into my chair, rubbing my fingers against my throbbing temples. I didn't need Matthew to tell me that the artwork was going to be late. I *knew* it was going to be late, if it even showed up at all.

What I didn't know was what to do about it.

Two years ago, I'd landed my dream job as assistant curator here at Halt, off the back of a successful kinetic exhibition I'd curated for the Tate Modern. But compared to some of the other curators – who'd been working at Halt so long they remembered when Warhol was just an upstart young commercial illustrator with a canned foods fetish – I was green. I'd been astounded when Matthew shoved a thick file on my desk two weeks ago and announced that it was my job to coordinate the exhibition details with Raynard.

My astonishment quickly turned to dread when I realised Raynard wasn't going to be easy to deal with. Despite his absurd insistence on an opening only a month away (most of our exhibitions at this scale were planned a year in advance) he refused to even get on the phone to discuss a single detail, and he had a list of demands rivalling that of a rockstar. He knew no gallery would turn down his wishes, and he was clearly a man of some considerable ego. Even though I greatly admired his work and I'd never even talked to the man, I was beginning to hate Ryan Raynard more and more each day.

Right now, my fear of losing my job boiled that hate over into seething, unadulterated rage.

Calm down, Alex. You have to think. I wiped my sweaty palms against my wool skirt. Perhaps Simon Host was just busy with other preparations for the exhibition. The exhibition was to be his client's first public showing in ten years, after all. It was likely Simon was in his office right now.

I dialled the number I now knew by heart, after calling it twenty times already today. While I listened to it ring, I refreshed my browser. No new emails. The phone rang and rang ... ten times ... twenty times ... Raynard's secretary still wasn't answering, and there was no way to leave a message.

What am I going to do?

This was the first major exhibit Matthew had entrusted me with. If I messed this one up, I'd be back to doing administration and running the children's gallery talks. If I had any hope of becoming a serious curator one day, I had to figure out a way to solve this.

My stomach churned. My pulse throbbed in my ears. I gulped down the urge to throw up. Panicking wasn't going to get those paintings to the gallery. I stared at my car keys on the table. There was nothing else to do.

I was going to talk to Ryan Raynard and make him hand over the artwork, even if it meant breaking into Raynard Hall itself.

2

ALEX

I sped out of the Halt Institute car park, and straight into a line of cars waiting to turn onto the high street. The radio blared out a news report about another hiker who'd been attacked by a rabid fox while walking in Crookshollow Forest. That was the third such incident this month. *Must be a global warming thing,* I thought, flicking the radio over to the local indie station. Greenies blamed global warming for everything, from unseasonably warm summers to lines at the supermarket.

I tapped my foot impatiently on the pedal, in my mind seeing Matthew's red face and curly moustache as he chewed me out. It was nearly 4pm, and traffic was starting to pick up for the afternoon, especially now that the tourist season was closing in. I needed to get across town to Raynard Hall as quickly as possible, so I could catch this Simon Host before he left the estate for the evening.

Like Salisbury and the Fens, Crookshollow Village and the surrounding forest was one of those English landscapes known for its ritual significance throughout history. There were several Neolithic henges and other ancient religious sites scattered across hilltops and hidden in the dense forest groves. Witches used to gather in the trees to dance naked and take part in ritual orgies – that was, until the witch finders swept in and put a stop to that. More than 200 convicted witches had been burnt in the market square at the opposite end of the high street, or at least that's the story they tell at the local medieval torture museum. It's said that the witches left their imprint in the landscape – that they transferred their spirits to their animal familiars, and their magic still dwells within the wild cats and foxes and deer and birds of Crookshollow Forest.

Growing up in the village, I was thrilled by these stories. They filled my imagination with enchanted worlds of witches and werewolves and fairies, right there in the forest on my own back doorstep. I was the weird loner kid, the strange girl who drew pictures all the time and sucked at playing cricket. After enduring days at school where kids either ignored me or threw things at me, I would take my paints and my camera and hike for miles into the gloom, stopping to draw fantastical scenes of witches dancing by the stream and half-human, half-crow creatures flying between the towering oaks. The forest fuelled my art and held together my soul.

But small towns were hell for kids like me, so I moved to London as soon as the final bell rang, eager to get away from the bad memories and embrace my art. I studied at the Wimbledon College of Arts, where I spent four blissful years painting and sculpting and attending political rallies and poetry readings and pretending to be a lamppost with eccentric performance artists. I lived in squalor and survived on white rice and kebabs. They were the best years of my life.

My carefree student days had to come to an end, and not just because my parents were killed in a car accident during my final year. I emerged a fresh-faced artist trying to establish myself right in the heart of the Global Financial Crisis. No one was buying art, especially not from an unknown like me. After six months of slogging my paintings around every independent gallery in

London, my landlady threatened me with eviction if I couldn't come up with the two months' rent I owed her.

I had to grow up and face facts: being an artist wasn't a viable career. I hadn't even been able to pick up a brush since my parents died. What kind of an artist was I, if I couldn't even paint through my pain? I had to find a real job.

Luckily, I was still in contact with my old professors, and through one of them, I landed a paid internship at the Tate Modern, then was offered a full-time position as a professional ass-kisser and errand-girl. I traded my paint-stained trackies for pencil skirts and pumps. My landlady stopped bugging me.

In the four years I worked at the Tate, I barely created any artwork, and I never hiked off into the wilderness. Even though I had a great job many people would've killed for, I felt like a failure. I wasn't turning into the person I always imagined myself to be. My kind, supportive parents who I usually turned to for advice were now just cold stones in a cemetery.

Still, the forest had called me back. When Halt offered me the job, I accepted without a second thought, packed up my apartment and moved into the tiny two-bed semi I shared with my friend Kylie, a pudgy calico cat named Miss Havisham and several recalcitrant mice. Our tiny back garden backed onto the forest edge.

I even started drawing and painting again, although I was woefully out of practice. Even though I lived near my parents' old house and all their memories, I felt calmer than I had in a long time. Except for today. Today I was so far from calm I couldn't see it if it were driving toward me in a Panzer tank.

I leaned on my horn as a woman wearing a kaftan covered with moon symbols stepped out from a candle shop and wandered across the street in front of the car, staring at her smartphone screen and completely unaware of the fact I'd had to slam on my brakes to avoid hitting her. It was all just another summer's day in Crookshollow.

Because of its significance as an ancient religious landscape, as well as being the site of numerous modern tales of hauntings, Crookshollow was a popular destination with free spirits and new-age pagans, all of whom were apparently on the road at *this very moment*, taking things as slowly as their pot-addled brains allowed. The centre of Crookshollow was a hodgepodge of occult stores, artisan candle makers, and alternative record shops, attracting a crowd with a particular disregard for traffic rules. The Halt building – a gleaming, modern installation of steel and glass, housing the art galleries, the witchcraft museum and some bank offices – loomed over the quaint high street, a constant reminder that corporate power still reigned supreme.

Eventually, I escaped the tangle of the high street and was speeding out toward Raynard Hall. Despite being back in Crookshollow for nearly two years, I hadn't travelled out near the crumbling manor since my childhood. I'd grown up in a small bungalow nearby, on Roundoak Drive, and the grounds of Raynard Hall were as familiar to me as my own childhood home.

Back then, the manor had been in the hands of Alistair Raynard, Ryan's father, who lived somewhere up in the Scottish mountains but kept on a few servants at the manor to maintain the estate. They never did a very good job. Overgrown and decaying, the manor had been a popular place for local kids to play, daring each other to approach the windows and peer in at the drab, empty rooms. Its dark stone façade, high gothic windows and sinister gargoyles lining the edge of the roof made it a popular source for local legends of ghosts and strange sightings. One of the most oft-told stories was of a younger Alistair Raynard – when he still lived in the Hall – hunting deer in the night and coming across a coven of witches in the forest. He was said to have chased them off his land with his rifle before they could complete their ritual and so they'd cursed him with some kind of affliction, and that was why he'd fled to Scotland.

I pulled into Holly Avenue. Raynard Hall dominated the view

– its towering grey turrets and black-shuttered windows casting a dim shadow across the bright townhouses that lined the street. A couple of tourists had parked their bikes at the gates and were snapping pictures of the famous artist's home, but they quickly moved on when they saw my car approach. I parked the car outside the heavy iron gates and stared up at the gothic manor, my breath catching in my throat. I'd walked past Raynard Hall hundreds of times as a kid, even sneaking into the grounds at night and peeking in at the grimy windows to see what ghosts might lurk inside, but it had never looked so menacing before.

I sucked in a breath. *You've got to do this, Alex. You need to call on all your hidden powers of persuasion and allure, and get inside that house. Or you can kiss your career at Halt goodbye.*

I leaned out the window and pushed the button on the intercom. It buzzed impatiently. My mind went completely blank. *What am I going to say? Ryan Raynard hasn't opened these doors to anyone else in ten long years. What will possibly make him open them for me?*

The intercom crackled, as if urging me to speak. I took a deep breath, then said, "Hello, Mr. Host? Mr. Raynard? I need to talk to someone about the exhibition—"

"Go away," a voice crackled on the other end. "This is private property."

I bristled. Who did this guy think he was? The haughty tone of Simon Host – coupled with my agitation at having being forced to stand outside the manor at all – made me snap back. "I'm parked on the road, *sir,* which is *not* private property at all, so I'd thank you to lose that tone and let me speak uninterrupted. I'm James Alexandra Kline, from the Halt Institute. I need to know when Ryan Raynard's paintings are being delivered. They should have arrived on Monday and we have a photographer waiting—"

"No one by that name lives here. Go away."

Now I was getting angry. "Do you think I'm an idiot? We've

talked on the phone several times already. Besides, who are you trying to fool? Ryan Raynard may be an artistic genius, but he's a idiot if he thinks he's flying below the radar living in a manor that would make the Addams Family jealous. How many gargoyles have you got on that façade? One ... two ... three ..." I counted them aloud. "*Fifteen* gargoyles. I mean, that's *obviously* the aesthetic choice of someone who wants to stay hidden away. I'm being sarcastic, in case you can't tell."

"I did ascertain that, thank you." The voice on the other end sounded faintly amused.

"Listen, Mr. Host, I know Raynard is inside that house, and I need to talk to him about the exhibit, and he's left me no other way to contact him. So either you let me in, or I cancel the exhibition. It's that simple."

My heart pounded against my chest. I hadn't planned to say all that. I'd got angry and it had all just slipped out, and now I wished I could take it back. I was taking a huge risk. Raynard could simply decide to cancel the exhibition, and my career would be over before it had even begun.

The intercom crackled. "What did you say your name was?"

"James Alexandra Kline. But people just call me Alex—"

"Very well. Drive up to the doors."

The gate creaked open, and I slammed down on the accelerator, careening up the cracked concrete drive before the voice on the end of the intercom could change his mind.

"Whoah." I gazed up at the imposing façade. Up close, the manor appeared even more sinister. It didn't look as if Ryan had done any upkeep on the place since he'd moved in. Weeds snaked across the drive from the wild, overgrown flower beds. Vines twisted around the columns flanking the main entrance. The glass on several windows was cracked or missing, and most were covered with thick, soiled drapes.

The dark oak front doors swung open, revealing a willowy man with beady eyes and a few wisps of grey hair, wearing an old-fashioned black tailored suit. He signalled to me to park off to the left, and follow him inside.

"I'm Alexandra Kline," I said, extending my hand to him. He merely stared at my outstretched digits, nodded, then walked silently through the lofty foyer. My cheap M&S pumps *clack-clacked* against the polished marble floor, and I couldn't help but glance around at the expensive, but dusty, furnishings and bland portraits in gilded frames that dominated the space.

The man led me down a wide hall, its vaulted ceiling painted with hunting scenes and framed by geometric designs. On the walls hung traditional portraits and hunting trophies – not the decor I'd expect from one of the foremost modern artists in Britain, whose paintings burst with light and movement and colour. I peered into the open rooms as we passed them, seeing some furnished with dark wood and thick velvet, others packed with boxes and furniture covered in white dust sheets, like silent ghosts of the manor's past.

This was the home of the great Ryan Raynard? It just didn't fit.

At the end of the hall we stepped into a cold drawing room, furnished with the same dark wood and heavy velvet drapery as the rest of the manor. It looked as if no one had used it for a long time, judging by the layer of dust covering every surface, and the spiderwebs clinging to the stag antlers hanging over the fireplace. The casement window was broken, and a chilly breeze blew from the overgrown garden behind the house and swirled around the room. I covered my bare arms with my hands, trying to keep them warm.

I turned to Raynard's Lurch, not certain what I was meant to do. "Where's Ryan?" I asked.

"I'll get you some tea," he croaked in reply, then shuffled away. I recognised his voice instantly. That was Simon Host.

Well, isn't this a walking bloody cliché? Raynard's secretary was also his butler. I perched gingerly on one of the grimy chairs, half expecting a bat to fly down from one of the darkened corners and materialise into Ryan Raynard before me. I pulled at a loose thread on my skirt, wishing I'd thought to go home and change into something smarter. My stomach twisted into a knot. I was about to meet the man whose art career I'd followed religiously since college, a man whose work made me see the world in new and exciting ways, who made me feel that wanting to make art was a perfectly legitimate and wonderful thing to do ...

I heard footsteps down the hall, and a deep voice calling out to the butler, who croaked out, "James Kline awaits your audience," from somewhere deeper in the house. The footsteps slowed as they approached the door, and the voice said, "Sorry about the wait, Mr. Kline. I've been busy in the studio. You know artists, always forgetting the time—"

Ryan Raynard stalked into the room, and I got my first glimpse of my artistic hero. He appeared younger than I expected, his unkempt red hair and stubbled chin at odds with the stiffness of the home around him. Deep, intelligent brown eyes flicked from object to object, unfocused, still lost in the world of whatever he'd been creating. He wore black jeans, a black vest pulled tight across his toned, sculpted chest, and heavy black motorcycle boots that clomped against the marble floor. All three of these items were splattered with paint.

Holy smokes. He was, in short, quite simply the most attractive man I'd ever laid eyes on. A strange shiver ran through my body, spreading from my head right down to my toes.

When Ryan finally looked up, his eyes met mine, and his whole body froze. The stiffness ran from his feet, right the way to the top of his head, as if someone had suddenly shoved a giant popsicle stick up his ass, forcing him upright. He opened his mouth as if to say something, but nothing came out.

I stood, my heart pounding, "Alex Kline," I said, outstretching my hand toward him, trying to keep my voice steady. "I'm from the Halt Institute. It's a pleasure to meet you, Mr. Raynard. I'm a huge fan of your work—"

Ryan Raynard stared at my hand hanging there in the space between us, with a look of such utter horror I had to turn it over to ensure it wasn't covered in grease or something.

"You ... you're a woman?" he whispered, his eyes boring into mine. The muscles in his face twitched, and I could see the veins in his neck standing out. Something was really wrong here.

"Last time I checked." My hand still hung awkwardly in the air. Ryan tore his gaze from mine, physically wrenching his body away from me. He backed away toward the door, his handsome face shot now with panic.

"Simon!" he yelled into the hall. "Come here, *now*!"

The butler rushed into the room, a tea tray clattering in his shaking arms. "Sir?"

Raynard was inching toward the door, his hard eyes glaring at me like I was a bug he wished to be squashed immediately. "Why did you let this ... this ...*woman* into my home? You know I don't want to be disturbed."

"You told me I could let her in, not five minutes ago, Mr. Raynard. She needs your paintings for the exhibition."

"You told me her name was James!"

"That's what she told me, sir—"

Ryan Raynard whirled around and faced me, his eyes burning. "You said your name was James."

I bristled, a sure-fire sign I was about to say something inappropriate. But he was acting like a jerk, so I allowed my voice to drip with scorn. "Forgive me; I didn't know my birth name had to be approved by the great Ryan Raynard. I was named after an ancestor on my mother's side, James Fauntelroy. Apparently, he used to help women accused of witchcraft in the village escape before they were trialled—"

"While I'm really enjoying this *fascinating* history lesson," Ryan faced into the hall so he didn't have to look at me, "you need to leave."

I shook my head, a stupid gesture, since he couldn't see me. "I can't leave until we've cleared up a few details for your exhibition. Where are the paintings? I know you've never done an exhibition before, so maybe all this organising is new to you, but if you want this one to go well, you need to cooperate with me. If I don't get those paintings to Halt tomorrow, the exhibition can't go ahead."

His shoulders sagged. I observed the movement with interest. It seemed the exhibition meant more to him than his attitude had led me to believe. "Simon, show Mrs. Kline—"

"Ms. Kline," I corrected him, cursing myself inwardly as I felt a blush appear on my cheeks. Luckily, Ryan was still avoiding my eyes, so he didn't see.

"—to the painting hall. Answer all her questions. If you want me, I'll be in the studio, but don't bring her in there. Please deal with Ms. Kline on all aspects concerning the exhibition, and make sure she understands that even though my paintings will be available to the public for the first time, I will not. *Don't* let anyone else in."

Without even another glance in my direction, Ryan Raynard slipped back into the hall and disappeared. The clomp of his boots faded away into silence.

Simon inclined his head toward me, indicating I should follow him. Picking myself up, I followed the butler out of the cold drawing room and back down that drab hall, through another dark, gloomy sitting room, and along a narrow corridor.

My whole body buzzed with a strange energy. It must've been the surge of righteous anger. *How dare he treat me like ... like I wasn't even a person, like I didn't even deserve his eye contact? No wonder he hides from the world, if he doesn't even have the decency to act pleasantly to those helping him. I can't believe that's the same guy who created all that beautiful art.*

"Is he always so ... abrasive?" I asked Simon, by way of making conversation. "How do you stand it?"

"Mr. Raynard has his proclivities," the butler replied, his drawn face indicating he thought he might have said too much.

"And what's his problem with women? This isn't the bloody Stone Age. Does he think the art world is only for straight, white, rich men like himself?"

The butler didn't reply.

We walked on in silence through the dark, drab hallway, Ryan's ancestors staring disapprovingly down on me. All the while I replayed the meeting with Ryan Raynard over in my mind – his handsome face hardening to stone when he realised I was female, his body going rigid like a statue, his aversion even to meet my eyes. The way he swaggered in, those gorgeous curls flopping in his eyes, his shoulders bulging from that black vest ...

I shook my head. Hot artistic visionary or not, the man was a complete tosser. It wouldn't do for me to dwell on his looks.

We stopped in front of a heavy steel door – at odds with the drab wood panelling that surrounded it. Simon hunched over the lock, keying in a complex combination. The door clicked open, and I was greeted with a sight that took my breath away.

A long, white room stretched in front of me, the other end a distant blur on the horizon. Rectangular skylights flooded the space in natural light, and after the gloom of the house, the light, airy space made me feel giddy, almost drunk. Simon flicked a switch, and rows of low-hanging spotlights flickered on, illuminating the artwork hanging on the walls. Every spare space on the walls was taken up with paintings – a hodgepodge of different styles and eras, all chosen with the keen eye of someone who understood colour and light and beauty. I noticed what looked like a Banksy print to the left of the door, butted up next to a Chagall. I turned, dizzy with the splendour of it all, and came face to face with some of Monet's water lilies, the beauty of the lines leaping from the canvas, pulling me into the gardens of Giverny, filling my nostrils with the scent of spring. I turned again, and this time my eye fell upon a Cézanne still life, the repetitive, exploratory brushstrokes creating a dramatic tension between the objects.

Nestled amongst these great works were pieces I recognised as belonging to the hand of Raynard himself. Impressionistic views of forests – great oaks with branches twisting, birds flying in lazy circles over a foggy grove, deer drinking from the brook. A beautiful red fox frolicking between the trees. I stepped closer, admiring the dappled light streaming from the gaps in the leaves, touching the fox's fur.

I glanced at the title. *Vixen.*

"Why isn't this painting in the exhibition?" I breathed. The title wasn't on the list Simon had given me. Ryan's exhibition was called *The Hunt,* and his images, we'd been informed, took inspiration from the animals in Crookshollow Forest as they went about their nocturnal wanderings. This remarkable piece should have been the focal point of the room.

Simon shook his head. "He will not part with that one for anything," he said. "And don't you even ask. Come, I have packaged up the ten pieces for the exhibition. Three of them are quite large, and I shall help you carry them to your car."

3

RYAN

hoa.
W I raced through the halls, my heart pounding, not stopping until I'd reached my studio. I slammed the door and sank against the wooden frame, willing my beating heart to return to normal.

I *knew* this exhibition was a bad idea. This is exactly what I'd been afraid would happen. I'd shut myself away from the world to avoid *exactly* this situation. For ten years I'd lived safely inside these walls, with everything I needed to be happy. And after Melissa, I'd sworn off women for good.

In one instant, it was all ruined. If Simon had told me the curator was a woman, I never would have gone out there, and I never would have discovered she was my vixen, my mate.

My mate.

The heat of her still coursed through my veins. I knew I'd been unforgivably rude, even for a guy who hadn't seen many women in his adult life. I'd just been so caught off guard by her presence, by her intoxicating, enchanting scent.

My legs were itching to run after her. I wanted to apologise to her, but of course if I tried to talk to her again, who knows what I might do?

I felt giddy, my veins coursing with lust. I couldn't trust myself around her, this Alexandra Kline. She could undo everything. She could undo me.

My head knew that taking a vixen was a terrible idea, but my body ... I had to fold my arms to suppress the urge to throw open the door, run back to her, and devour those gorgeous lips. I wanted to slam her against a wall and fuck her senseless. I wanted to drown in those huge, penetrating eyes, feel those long legs wrapped around my back as I drove deep inside her ...

No. I balled my hands into fists, closing my eyes and beating on my thighs until the urges passed. *You can't have her. You have to be strong. You are not destined to have a mate. You are supposed to remain alone. Alone is safe for everyone, especially her.*

You have to get through this exhibition, and then if you never see Alexandra again, the feeling will pass. She doesn't want you anyway. She now thinks you're an obnoxious twat, and with good reason.

You have to forget about her.

I opened my eyes, casting my gaze around the manor's ballroom, which I'd converted into a large studio. Light streamed from the skylights I'd had cut into the high ceilings, casting interesting shadows on the elaborate plaster detailing. The marble floor shimmered beneath my feet. In the centre of the room, the white grand piano was covered with canvases stretched across easels. Benches sat beside the floor-to-ceiling windows, overlooking the gardens and forest below. Lamps stood scattered throughout the room, bent at odd angles to create the exact lighting effects I wanted to recreate in my paintings. Shelves and boxes of paints and supplies lined one wall, beneath a large mural depicting a wild fox hunt – the only remnant of the room's previous purpose.

Usually, just being in this space gave me comfort, but not now. My blood ran hot, a fire coursing through my veins.

My current work-in-progress waited for me at my easel beneath a modern, industrial chandelier, but just looking at it made me agitated. I snatched a handful of salted peanuts from the bowl beside my palette, and shoved them in my mouth. My tastebuds exploded with salt.

You have to stay calm. There's a way to fix this.

So my mate had appeared. Big deal. So this miraculous event happened at the worst possible time. I could handle it. Judging from her reaction, Alexandra didn't know what she was, what *we* were. Which meant that in time, she'd forget me. She'd move on. And as long as *they* never found out about her, Alexandra wouldn't be in any danger.

Just because my body craved her, didn't mean I had to give in. Simon was handling all the preparations for the exhibition. I wouldn't have to encounter this woman again. I'd just stay locked away in my castle and hope it all blew over.

Everything could go on as planned. It would all be fine.

Logically, I knew all this was true. So why did I have a sinking feeling in my gut that this was only the beginning of my problems?

4

ALEX

It was well past 8 p.m. by the time Simon and I had packed the paintings into the car and the iron gates of Raynard Hall had creaked shut behind me. I drove home, my stomach fluttering nervously every time I glanced in the rearview mirror and saw the stack of precious Ryan Raynard paintings jostling about in the backseat.

As I drove, I replayed my encounter with Ryan over and over again in my mind. He certainly was a strange man. How could he be so cold and neanderthalic, and yet paint such emotional and harmonious scenes? What was with his aversion to me being female? Could an artist as young and handsome as he was really be as chauvinistic as that?

I drove home to my flat. The Halt building would be shut up tight for the night, and although I could enter the main building after hours, I didn't have security access to the gallery spaces or the warehouse, which were high-security zones. Only Matthew and Gavin – the head exhibition technician – had after-hours access to those areas. Gavin wasn't answering his phone, and I didn't exactly want to pull Matthew away from watching *Coronation Street* in his pyjamas – or whatever it was he did in the evenings – to get him to unlock it for me. Our flat had a decent security system (you had to, in our neighbourhood). The paintings would be safe enough in my flat for the night.

Once I was home, Kylie helped me carry the crates upstairs. Our staircase was so narrow that it took some serious twisting to get the larger canvases around the corner on to the upper landing. Every time the corner of a canvas bumped against the wall, I lost a few years off my life.

By the time all ten crates were stacked in the upstairs hallway, my nerves were completely shot. We dumped out all my clothing onto the bed and stacked the paintings into my wardrobe.

"It looks like you've already got some paintings back here," said Kylie, as she pulled out a large square of canvas wrapped in brown paper and a wooden frame, similar to the way Simon had packaged Ryan's pieces.

Heart racing, I snatched the canvas from her hands. "That's nothing. Don't worry about those," I said. "Just leave them back there and stack these on top."

The previous tenants had attached a bolt to the outside of the wardrobe. For what purpose I could only guess. Did they punish a naughty child by locking them away? Were they afraid their shoes were going to walk out in the night and strangle them in their sleep? Regardless of the reasoning, the bolt came in handy tonight.

"Now I just need something to lock it with," I said, leaning against the door and staring at my tiny room, the walls crammed with artwork and the bed piled high with dresses and jackets and shoes. What a strange day this was turning into.

"I've got it!" Kylie scampered downstairs, returning a few minutes later with her bicycle lock.

"Don't you need that so thugs won't steal your bicycle?"

Kylie shrugged as she fitted the lock on the door. "I am no longer a cyclist. On Monday, I cycled home from Crooks Crossing in the rain, and a bird shat on my shoulder. I'm back to being a gas-guzzling air polluter, just like you. I'm secretly hoping my bike *will* get stolen so I can claim it on my insurance and buy some new shoes."

We shoved a heavy chest in front of the closet, for good measure. I sat on my bed amongst my Fluevog boots and vintage rock tees, staring at that wardrobe door; unable to believe I had ten Ryan Raynard paintings just sitting in there. The urge to open them up and look at them was practically unbearable, but I knew that was risking too much to even attempt. My eyes flicked across the room to where my easel was set up with a canvas half finished – a moonscape painted through the trees outside my window. Quickly, I leaned across the bed and flipped it over, so Kylie couldn't see it. She didn't even notice.

With the exception of my parents, my art teachers at university and the gallery owners I'd failed to impress, I'd never shown anyone else my work; not even Kylie, who was probably the closest friend I'd ever had. I didn't turn to art as much as I had in university, but there were times – usually after a bad breakup, or after Matthew had dressed me down in front of everyone at the office – where I would sit at the easel for hours, slashing at the canvas with pen and brush as though it were a carcass to be butchered. I had boxes of sketchbooks and journals under the bed, as well as those finished canvases packaged up in the wardrobe, hidden away from the cruel eyes of the world.

Years working in gallery management had now fully shattered my dreams of being a working artist. I wasn't in anywhere near the same league as those guys. They were big thinkers, dreamers, and escapists operating outside the normal plane of existence, usually with family money or major investors behind them. I was a realist, with rent and car payments and a Fluevog habit. I needed the nine-to-five.

Ryan Raynard painted because painting was how he became who he was. When I painted, I did it to become, for a few hours, someone other than myself.

Disappointment surged through me. *If only Ryan hadn't been such an arsehole.* I would have loved to just sit with him and talk, even for ten minutes. I had so many questions about his work, so much I wanted to say about how he'd inspired me. *This is exactly why they say you should never meet your idols.* Tears itched my eyes, but I forced them back. So he'd shattered my illusions. Whatever. It wasn't as if that was the first time that had ever happened to me.

Kylie saw the expression on my face. "You need wine," she said, grabbing my hand and pulling me downstairs.

I slumped down onto our couch, my fingers tugging at the loose stitching holding the overstuffed cushions together. I could call the couch 'vintage', but that would be overly generous. It was simply old; pilfered from the side of the road where a resident on Roundoak Drive had been clearing out their junk, it now hosted a collection of mysterious stains left over from wine and cheese evenings that had gone on until the early hours, and tufts of stuffing falling out where Miss Havisham used it as a scratching post.

In our tiny kitchen, Kylie pulled a bottle of white wine from the fridge and poured two glasses. She set mine down in front of me, and next to it, placed a tub of mint chocolate chip ice cream, with two large spoons. My stomach growled. I'd spent so long collecting the paintings I hadn't eaten any dinner. I pulled off the top off the tub and scooped a large spoonful into my mouth.

"So." Kylie slumped down in the chair opposite and dug in with her own spoon. Miss Havisham jumped up on her lap and gave her wine glass an experimental bat. "Talk. What happened today? Why am I helping you stash priceless paintings in your wardrobe? Did you finally get tired of working for that asshole Matthew Callahan and decide to heist the place?"

In between scoops of ice cream, I filled her in on Matthew's outburst, my visit to Raynard Hall, and my meeting with the infamous Ryan Raynard. Kylie's eyes widened when I told her about Ryan's reaction to my presence.

"That's so strange," Kylie mumbled, her mouth full of ice cream. "It's almost as if he was afraid to be in the same room as you."

I shrugged. "I don't want to waste any of my energy trying to puzzle out why he acted like he did. As far as I'm concerned, the guy is a misogynist prick, and that's the end of it."

"No one else has been inside that house, Alex, not for ten years. But you got in. Maybe Mr. Ryan Raynard isn't as opposed to your presence as you think."

Against my better judgement, I wished that were true. The memory of Ryan walking in the room, broad shoulders held high and clothing dishevelled from the studio flashed before my eyes. My body pulsed with energy at the thought of what that body might feel like pressed up against mine. A shudder of delight ran through my body, the way it had done when he'd first entered the room. I'd never felt anything like it before.

Of course you're lusting after him. This guy is one of your idols, and you've just found out he's completely smoking hot. The idea that he might find you special is always going to appeal. You're acting like a rockstar groupie. Now, cut it out.

I could feel my cheeks growing hot. "Don't make me choke on my own scorn, Kylie. He only let me in because my first name is James and he thought he was talking to a man, the only gender capable of understanding his artistic vision."

Kylie wrinkled her nose. "Oh, right. That. Never mind how you got in, Alex. Ryan is a celebrity, and a mysterious and sexy one, at that. You could sell your story to a trashy tabloid for a million pounds, and you'd never have to work again. That would get him back for treating you badly."

She had a point, but I shook my head. "They'd want to make out that I slept with him or something. And there's no way I want *that* following me around."

"If he's anything like as hot as you describe, it wouldn't be a bad thing." Kylie licked her lips.

No, it most certainly would not.

Shut up. I couldn't believe the things my brain was thinking today. *Who are you, anyway, some horny university student?*

"Kylie!" I blushed as she smirked, then shrugged. "He hates women." I said furiously, the flush in my face growing hotter. "All the tabloid money in the world wouldn't get me to even pretend-sleep with an arrogant prick like Ryan Raynard. Now, can we drop it?" I held out my glass for another refill. "How was your day?"

"Strange," she said. Kylie was a nurse at Crooks Crossing General Hospital, in the next town over. Her work stories were often filled with vivid characters and tough, tenacious doctors I always imagined looking like George Clooney. "We have another girl in the ICU after being bitten by a fox. They think she's going to be okay, but the police were there most of the day, grilling her and her hiking partner for information. They've got some hair-brained plan to trap this fox before it gets anyone else. If it's as out-of-control as they think it is, it could kill someone."

"Oh, yeah? Good on them. I heard about the hiker on the radio. Is it true that the fox is rabid?"

"It doesn't seem to be rabies, but there's definitely something unusual about the bites. The patients are exhibiting strange reactions, but they're trying to keep that out of the press. What you wouldn't have heard about is the man I've got under observation with three cracked ribs and some nasty bruising around his chest. He claims he was rammed by a deer. But deer don't do that." Kylie wrinkled up her nose again. "It's all very strange."

"Indeed." We'd both had strange days. At least we had wine – the one guaranteed cure for any of life's disappointments. I finished my glass and reached across the table for the bottle. "Another?"

5

RYAN

The agitation from Alexandra Kline's visit still coursed through my veins. I'd given up painting hours before. The image just wasn't flowing the way I wanted it to. It didn't help that Alexandra's gorgeous face kept floating in front of my eyes. If I wasn't careful, I'd end up painting her into the piece, and I knew from experience how well *that* turned out.

Only one thing would cure me of this itch.

"I'm going out," I announced to Simon at dinner. He'd outdone himself, with steak cooked to perfection, buttery garlic potatoes, and steamed beans. I think he was trying to make up for letting Alexandra in the house.

"Are you sure that's such a good idea?" Simon asked from his position behind my chair, where he hovered in case I needed my napkin folded or my wine refilled. Simon came from a long line of butlers who'd served my family. He was my father's butler before me. He liked to observe all the traditions of his post. I used to force him to eat at the table with me, but he'd been so uncomfortable I'd finally just given in and let him do his hovering thing.

"No, it's probably not. Regardless, I feel the need to get some air. Don't worry." I held my glass up, and he stepped forward to fill it. "I'll be careful."

"Very well, sir."

As soon as I'd cleared my plate, I stepped out the backdoor. Simon had already scanned the area with the high-tech surveillance equipment in his office, and declared no reporters were lurking in the trees. I was safe, for now.

I stood on the cobbles, looking out over the overgrown garden – the wide avenues of yew, the mazes of pathways and flowerbeds stretching down the slope of the hill, finishing right on the edge of the forest – a boundary between the overbearing human world, and the freedom of the wild.

I raised my chin to the heavens, and forced my shift, calling up the fox within me. He answered instantly. My bones crunched loudly as they cracked and rearranged themselves. I sucked in my breath, willing myself to endure the pain of it as I had done so many times before. I dropped onto my hands and knees, my back arching as my ribcage shifted forward, my vertebrae re-aligned to my new figure. I stared at the cobbles beneath me, watching my fingers transform into paws and dark red fur poke through my skin to cover my arms.

My face tugged in every direction, as my human features were pulled apart, to be remade again as the fox. My vision swirled, changing into a world of black and white, a world where scents painted the landscape with all kinds of wondrous new sensations.

I shook out my fur, admiring my bushy tail. Even after all these years, it still took me a few minutes after my shift was complete to get used to working that tail.

The change completed, I took off through the garden, quickening my pace as I entered the forest. I broke into a run, darting through the trees, relishing the new scents and sounds as they rushed at me. The forest swelled around me, alive with possibility.

This is exactly what I needed – to be here, in the woods, where I could be truly free. All I had to do was get Alexandra out of my mind, and make it through this exhibition, and everything would be fine.

Well, not fine, exactly, but better than it was now.

If only my body would stop calling for her. I could still feel her in my veins, a heat that rushed through my body, quickening my heart. In my fox form, the heat was even worse. Even though I didn't want a mate, the hands of fate clearly delighted in playing this ridiculous cosmic joke on me.

If only I could—

A scent wafted across my nose, causing all thoughts of Alexandra Kline to fly from my mind.

Marcus.

He was here. He'd moved into my territory.

It was beginning.

I stopped in my tracks, placing my snout to the ground, and working out the trail from the maze of crisscrossed paths. He wasn't alone; there was another shifter with him – a bran, I figured, judging by the heady bird scent.

A faint tingle of fear rushed along my spine, making my tail flap against the ground. If Isengrim was making his first forays into my territory, it meant I didn't have much time left. But why send only Marcus? At best, we were evenly matched. What was going on?

Alexandra. She's what's going on.

I followed the trail through the trees for half a mile, my agitation growing with every step. It was him all right, and he was heading toward the village, which couldn't be a good thing. Marcus showing up here the very day I encounter my mate couldn't be a coincidence.

I didn't want to see Alexandra Kline again. If I got within a few feet of her, all my shifter senses would take over, and I'd be helpless to resist. But clearly, the universe had other plans. I wouldn't let an innocent woman get caught up in this battle, especially not the woman who was supposed to be mine.

I lowered my head again, and bounded back toward Crookshollow. *I'll find you yet, you bastard. You stay away from her.*

6

ALEX

After Kylie and I polished off both the tub of ice cream and the bottle of wine, I brushed my teeth, changed into an oversized t-shirt featuring the logo of my art-school boyfriend's black metal band, and crawled into bed. Miss Havisham curled up beside my feet, and soon she was snoring peacefully.

I, however, couldn't sleep. My thoughts kept drifting to Ryan Raynard's piercing eyes, and those paintings locked in the wardrobe. I was an idiot. I should have called Matthew and taken them into the museum. It was crazy of me to store them here, even for one night. Those paintings were worth *millions*. What if Kylie decided she needed a midnight snack and accidentally burned the house down? What if mice ate through the wooden boxes and nibbled on the edges? What if the roof leaked during the night and soaked them through? If those paintings suffered so much as a scuff, both Matthew and Ryan Raynard would have my head, and that was not a fun prospect. I was rather attached to my head.

I'd arranged my room so the bed was pushed up against the back wall, directly underneath the window, with my easel and overflowing washing basket at the foot. I leaned over and pushed the window open, listening to the wind as it whistled through the trees, shaking the leaves and rubbing the bent oak branches up against the side of the flat. An owl hooted. I sucked in a deep breath of that fresh air. The forest always calmed me. *Everything is going to be fine. You'll take the paintings into work tomorrow, Matthew will be pleased, and Tara will have to wipe that smirk off her face—*

Outside the window, a twig snapped.

My heart pounded. *It's just a fox, or a deer. Don't worry about it.*

Without thinking, my gaze fell on the locked wardrobe door, my thoughts flying to the priceless paintings hidden inside.

Another snap. I pulled back from the window, my heart pounding. Was it burglars? The exhibition was making headlines all over the world. It would be easy for someone to find my name in one of the articles and follow me when I left Halt. They would've seen me enter Raynard Hall and come out with the paintings. Given Ryan's reputation, these paintings would fetch a tidy sum on the black market. There could be any number of unscrupulous characters ready to take advantage of any weakness in our security. *Why did I not think of this? Why didn't I call Matthew, like I should have?*

Stupid. You're so stupid, Alex. You always make snap decisions, and they're always, always the wrong ones.

I forced my panic back down into my gut. I lay down on my stomach and used my elbows to pull my body closer to the window. I rested my head on the sill and leaned out, my eyes struggling to see in the dim moonlight.

Below me, in the garden, more twigs snapped. I heard a whispered voice. *Fuck, fuck, fuck!* It wasn't just my imagination. Someone was out there.

Leaves crunched, and the branches beneath the window swayed as a black shadow darted across the garden. Someone was climbing up the oak tree against the back of the flat, the tree that led straight to my bedroom window. It looked like an animal the way it moved, but I knew no animal that large would come this close to the house, let alone try to climb the oak tree under my window.

My heart pounded against my chest. I rolled away from the window, accidentally kicking Miss Havisham awake. She meowed in protest, lifted her head, sniffed the air, and raced off into the dark house. Cats are much smarter than humans.

Outside the window, a crow squawked ... a carrion bird signalling my doom.

Panic rose in my chest, threatening to freeze me in place. *Focus, Alex.* I needed a weapon. I cast my gaze around the room. Unless I could clobber the intruder to death with one of my fluevogs, I had nothing. There were knives in the kitchen, but could I get there in time? I doubted it.

I know! Kylie's boyfriend Ray was a medieval re-enactor, and he kept all his gear at our place since he didn't have room in his mum's basement, which was where he lived (yes, Ray was a real winner). I was forever tripping over his enormous broadsword on the way to the bathroom.

His broadsword. Perfect.

As silently as I could, I pulled myself out of the bed and crawled along the floor toward the door, thinking that they might not be able to see me through the window if I stayed low. As I did most nights, I'd kept my bedroom door open a crack so Miss Havisham could come and go from my bed to her bowl in the kitchen. Now I pulled back the door open wide enough so I could crawl through. It let out a mighty creak, the sound like a gunshot in my ears. I held my breath. *Please don't let the intruder hear that.*

I listened. I couldn't hear anything inside the house or out. I dared to hope that maybe they'd gone. But then ... in the void of darkness, something went *click* downstairs ... and then a metal sliding. Someone was pulling open one of the living room windows. They must have decided to abandon the tree.

My heart pounding in my chest, I crawled as silently as I

could into the hallway, feeling in front of me with my hands for the bag of reenactment gear Ray kept at the top of the stairs. My hand grasped something hard. A leather handle. *Yes.* Never again would I give Ray a hard time about being a *Dungeons & Dragons* freak.

I heard a thud from downstairs. Any second now, the burglars could come up to the bedrooms. I fumbled with the bag, pushing aside leather gauntlets, foam swords, and an elven cloak, before my hand clasped the hilt of a long, heavy sword. I lifted it from the bag, pulled off the leather scabbard, and held it in front of me the way I'd seen Ray do it; both hands clasped on the hilt beside my hip, with the tip pointing upward toward my invisible opponent's face. The blade was blunt – designed for reenactment – but it would still cause a great deal of pain. I pressed my back against the wall, my eyes on the dark stairwell, while Miss Havisham circled around my feet.

Now what? Did I wait up here for them to come up the stairs and around the corner, or did I go downstairs and make the first move? I saw a light flickering from the stairwell, and heard a glass shatter in the kitchen. A man swore.

They certainly weren't being subtle. If they came up here in the dark, would I be able to hit them? Or would they – with their superior breaking-and-entering skills – simply overpower me? Would I be better to take them by surprise downstairs, where I might have a better shot at making the door if I got into trouble?

Miss Havisham, using cat logic to discern that anyone banging around in the kitchen in the middle of the night was obviously there to bring her a second dinner, bounded down the stairs. *Right then, I guess I'm going down. Thank you, kitty.*

I pressed my back against the wall and slid, inch after terrified inch, around the corner down the narrow staircase, the sword pointed across my body and the point at eye level for anyone trying to climb up. I heard cupboard doors being slammed, packages torn open, things being smashed against the floor.

And I heard something else ... a low, mean growl. *What? Did they bring a dog, too?* This was just looking worse and worse.

No turning back now. I paused at the bottom of the stairs, the sword point peeking out into the front hall. I could hear footsteps in the living room, heavy breathing as someone rifled through the couch cushions. I needed to peek around the corner and see what was happening so that I could plan my move. I sucked in a breath, and stretched my neck out, straining to see around the corner without moving from my spot.

A tall man with jet-black hair that hung down to his shoulders, framing a gaunt, bony face and long hooked nose, bent over my coffee table, sifting through the empty crisp packets and trashy magazines obscuring the surface. His brow furrowed in concentration as he picked up each magazine or piece of trash and shook it, watching to see if something fell out. He tossed the empty ice cream tub into the corner in disgust. Before I could stop her, Miss Havisham raced from the stairs after it, mewling with delight.

The black-haired man looked up, and recoiled in disgust when he saw the cat streak across the floor in front of him. He backed around the other side of the sofa, closer to me, as he sought to put some distance between himself and Miss Havisham, who was oblivious to his presence as she tried to hook the ice cream tub out from under the tea trolley with her paw. The man made a clicking noise with his throat, almost like a bird in distress.

This man broke into our flat while we were still inside, and he's afraid of a cat?

Another man walked into the room from the kitchen, holding a raw chicken drumstick in his hand. He had sandy hair with a slight reddish tinge, and although he was shorter than his fellow felon, he was broader across the shoulders, his athletic frame completely blocking the kitchen doorway. He wore a tight black t-shirt that showed off every curve of his toned chest. His facial features seemed vaguely familiar, but I didn't usually associate with raw-food criminals, so I couldn't think where I might've seen him before.

The sandy-haired man kicked at a magazine on the ground. "What are you reading those for? The paintings aren't here. They're too heavy for the girl to move upstairs on her own. I reckon she's hidden them somewhere else."

"But we traced them back here!"

"She might have tricked us. I've watched the girl – she's not an idiot."

The black-haired man held up the cover of a *Cosmo* magazine, and punched the page. "Are you sure about that, Marcus? This is what's she's reading."

The man in the kitchen – Marcus – took a bite out of the chicken leg ... just tore a chunk of raw chicken off with his teeth, and chewed on it, smacking his lips together loudly. *What was going on here?*

"You're disgusting." The man named Edgar scowled. *No arguments there.*

"You're just jealous that you didn't find the freezer first," Marcus smirked, as he took another bite. "Shall we?" He gestured to the window.

"We haven't got what we came for." Edgar frowned. "She'll have them under her bed or something. We should look there."

"Look at that staircase," Marcus gestured. I yanked my head back as the black-haired man's head swung around, then peered out again as his gaze moved past my hiding spot. "She wouldn't be able to fit them up the stairs without damaging them. They're priceless paintings. Isengrim is wrong; she'd have locked them up somewhere safe. This whole evening is a waste of our time. We've achieved what we came for. The place is a mess. She's going to know that it's important for her to stay away from the young Raynard. If you want to really ensure she gets the message, we could kill the cat and write something atrocious like 'stay away from Ryan Raynard' on the wall in its blood."

"Please?" Edgar squawked, raising his hands and curling his fingers in the air. I saw he wore black nail polish on his long nails, each one sharpened to a point, like talons. I tightened my grip on the sword. *They aren't going to touch my kitty. Not if I have anything to say about it. And why are they talking about Ryan as if they know him?*

"I'm not touching it," Marcus growled, the words coming from deep in his throat. He tossed the chicken leg into the corner. Miss Havisham leapt on it, and began licking at the frozen meat. Marcus lifted his chin and sniffed deeply, screwing up his face in a grotesque expression. "It's a *cat*. Its smell is repugnant—"

His words were cut off abruptly when a giant fox – at least the size of a large dog – leapt in through the open window and sank his teeth into Marcus' leg.

What the—

I jumped so high, I banged my head on the top of the stairs, and nearly dropped my sword.

"Yeeow!" Marcus cried, as the force of the attack sent him flying against the wall. He grabbed the fox around the neck and tried to pull it off his leg, but the animal hung on tenaciously, shaking Marcus' leg as it dug its teeth in deeper. It was the largest fox I'd ever seen, its fine red coat shining in the dim light as it fought to keep its grip on the intruder, splattering blood across the linoleum. Its long, bushy tail lashed back and forth, knocking a stack of CDs and Kylie's decorated plate collection off the top of the cabinet. I don't know what had compelled it to jump into the house like that, but I wasn't going to waste this chance.

I hope it's not the rabid fox that's been biting people in the forest ...

Not stopping to contemplate that thought further, I sprung from behind the stairs and rushed at Edgar, holding my sword out in front of me, point aimed at his face. He turned toward me and held up his hands, his face wide with shock. I didn't falter.

My blade collided with his face, hitting him in the cheekbone with all the force of my body behind it. He spun and collapsed against the sofa.

I lifted the blunt blade above my head, and brought it down as hard as I could on his back. I heard it crunch as it connected with bone, and he cried out and thrashed out his arms. "Get out of my house!" I screamed. "And don't you *dare* touch my cat!"

I raised the sword to hit him again, but when I brought it down, the man seemed to shrink back into his clothes, his arms and legs fading into nothing, leaving only empty jeans and his black t-shirt draped over the cushions.

Now I knew that wasn't normal. *What was going on?*

I picked up the corner of the t-shirt, but there was nothing underneath except air. Edgar was gone. Somewhere in my house was a naked intruder, probably on his way to my bedroom. The thought made me shudder. I whirled around, but couldn't see or hear anyone on the stairs.

Where had he gone? How did he *do* that?

I kicked the jeans to the ground. A big black raven flew out of them. I screamed, dropping the broadsword and closing my hands to catch the bird as it came at me. It squawked angrily as it landed on my fingers, wings flapping madly as it clawed at my skin, trying to get through my hands to peck out my eyeballs. Its sharp talons dug into the palm of my hand.

"Argh!" I spun around, slamming the bird against the wall. It let go of my hand and dropped to the floor, dazed. I kicked at it, but it skittered out of the way, hopped through the living room and dived for the open window.

The bird now taken care of, I turned – clutching my injured, bleeding hand – to the man and fox crashing around the kitchen. But the man was no longer there. In his place, a giant, sandy-coloured fox fought against the other reddish one. On the floor between them lay the black t-shirt and jeans the sandy-haired intruder had worn.

Okay, now this is out of control.

Plates crashed from the shelves as the red fox slammed the other against the oven, baring its teeth and snarling menacingly. The sandy one snapped back, raising a paw and swiping at his opponent's face, leaving a shallow scratch across the red fox's cheek. The red fox went for the neck, but a roasting dish slipped from the top of the oven and clattered on its head, momentarily dazing it.

Sensing its chance, the sandy fox slipped under the red fox's grip and dived for the window. The red fox sped after it, snapping at its hind legs, but the red fox was still a little dazed, and the sandy fox scrambled free. The red fox turned to me, its large brown eyes giving me a look that said, "I'm sorry," and then it too leapt through the window.

Kylie came running down the stairs. "What happened?" she cried, casting her eyes around the mess. "I heard crashing and voices—"

"Shut the window!" I cried as I yanked open the front door and ran – barefoot, wearing only my ex-boyfriend's band t-shirt – into the night. My feet stung as they hit the cold concrete of our front walk, and my heart pounded against my chest as I pumped my arms and tried to pour on enough speed to catch up to the foxes. They ran down the centre of the deserted street, their lithe bodies silhouetted in the moonlight. Down the road, the red fox chased the sandy fox, leaping and snarling at its heels, at each step only inches from taking a bite.

Are they rabid? Please don't let them be rabid.

As they reached the end of the cul-de-sac, the sandy fox turned and faced its foe, pulling back its lips and baring its teeth as it snarled, deep and vicious. The red fox moved between the sandy fox and me, holding its ground, staring down the enemy. The sandy fox snarled again, and I raised my hands to my face, ready to turn and run if it became a bloodbath. But then, the sandy fox turned and stalked off down a driveway, into the forest.

The red fox darted to the edge of the driveway, barking after its sandy-furred foe. Not wanting to be seen by a creature that might have rabies, I ducked into the nearest yard and peered through a bush, feeling in my gut that if I stayed close, I'd get to the bottom of this strange night.

As I stood behind the bush and watched, the giant red fox stared up at the moon, and barked once. At first, I thought I was imagining its snout decreasing, its hind legs lengthening, its tail shrinking back into its body. But then, as I watched in awe, the creature rose up on two legs, its torso stretching and reshaping and becoming something new. In a matter of seconds, there was no longer a fox standing in the centre of the cul-de-sac, but a tall, naked man with wavy red hair.

A man I recognised.

"Ryan Raynard?"

I clamped my hands over my mouth, but it was too late. He turned toward my voice, his face a mixture of fear and anger. It was no good hiding from him. I stepped out from behind the bush, and took a tentative step toward the very muscled, very tense, very *naked* figure of Ryan Raynard, his red hair almost glowing under the moonlight. His shoulders sagged ever so slightly.

"You saw," he said. It wasn't a question.

7

RYAN

Alexandra Kline stared at me, her beautiful eyes wide with shock and awe. I didn't blame her. I'd have stared at someone the same way if I'd just seen them transform from a fox into a human.

Dammit, so close.

I should have guessed she'd follow me. From what little I knew about this woman, she was clearly not above rushing head-first into potentially harmful situations, like confronting her most prestigious artist when he was being a prick, and rushing Edgar with that sword ... I mean, where had she got a *sword* from? She was certainly an intriguing woman—

Stop it. My body thrummed with energy, the pull of our connection threatening to overwhelm me. I tried to tear my eyes away from Alexandra, to break the spell she had over me, but I found myself at a loss. Those wide, brown eyes, those red, kiss-able lips ...

A strand of her hair fell over her face, and my fingers itched to brush it away, to make that first skin-on-skin contact that would pull us both under. But I had to resist. Alexandra was a complication, yes, but I wouldn't allow myself to get distracted with another woman. Not again, and especially not now.

It was better to be alone. That way, no one else got hurt. And looking at that stunning woman cowering behind the rosebush, I wanted nothing more than to protect her from pain, even if that meant protecting her from me.

Which meant that right now I had to come up with an explanation for why I was standing out here, stark naked.

"What's going on, Ryan?" Alexandra's head stuck out from behind a bush. Her eyes flashed. "What are you doing here? Why were there men and animals in my house? How did you ...?" She left the question hanging, unable to articulate just what she'd just seen. She lowered her gaze, staring intently at the neighbour's rose bushes.

Go on, Ms. Kline. Ask me how I transformed from a red fox into a naked man. Ask me what I was doing in your house.

I sighed. I'd give her one last chance to enable her to go back to her life without getting caught up in this mess. If she was smart, she'd take it.

"I go for walks at night sometimes around Crookshollow," I said lamely. "I gather inspiration for my paintings while I'm unlikely to meet tourists or art groupies along the paths. I happened to be walking past your house when I saw those men enter, and I thought I'd better try to help. I didn't even realise it was your house, Alexandra. Unfortunately, by the time I had run into the street and called the police, that fox had chased them away."

I knew from the way she shuffled her foot against the dirt that she didn't believe me. I couldn't blame her. It wasn't a particularly good excuse. But she could take it and turn away and that would be the end of everything.

"Call me Alex. The police aren't coming, are they, Ryan?" She took a step backward, then another, her eyes making a subtle jerk back down the street. Her muscles tensed. Any moment now she would bolt back toward her flat.

I shook my head. "I knew you wouldn't fall for that story."

Alex took another step backward. "It was a pretty dumb story. I need a real answer. Why are you naked, Ryan? Do you just wander around the neighbourhood starkers?" She folded her arms across her stunning breasts. "I've met some pretty eccentric artists at Halt, but this really takes the prize."

I switched tactics, settling on wheedling. "Alex, please ... I promise I'll explain everything, but could we do it inside?"

"You want to come *inside* my house? After you show up here naked and ... whatever you are. How do I know you aren't some kind of creepy stalker?"

I smirked, opening my arms wide. "If I was a creepy stalker, where would I keep my long-range camera? My night-vision goggles?"

"I can suggest a place," she shot back. I grinned despite myself. Damn, this woman was going to be tough to forget.

"Please, Alex. Let me sit down inside and I'll explain."

"Could you maybe ... put your pants back on first?"

"Are you sure about that?" I grinned. Immediately, I snapped the grin off my face. Why was I *flirting* with her? I didn't want to flirt with her. That had just slipped out.

Shit. This was going to be harder than I thought.

Her voice came out hard. "Oh yes. I'm sure."

Good, at least one of us knew we were a bad idea. I knew I definitely deserved her derision. I had treated her like crap back at the Hall, and now, thanks to me, Marcus and Edgar had trashed her apartment. "As you wish."

She turned away from me and started walking back toward the flat, watching me over her shoulder. Luckily, we'd stopped near one of my caches. I walked over to the house at the end of the street, and pulled a bundle wrapped in plastic out of their bushes. I could feel Alex's eyes on me as I unwrapped a complete change of clothes, including underwear, jeans, a blue shirt, and a pair of Italian shoes.

Slowly, deliberately, I pulled everything on, angling my body so she couldn't see my crotch. My cock wasn't behaving. I was desperate to forget this woman, and it was throbbing against my leg. Just knowing Alex was *watching* me was already turning me on. We hadn't even touched, and the connection shot through my body like an electrical socket. I'd need a cold shower before the night was through.

I hated to think what would happen if we ever did happen to touch.

If we touched ...

The urge to do it coursed through me. If I touched her, I would mark her as mine, officially. By vulpine law that would give me additional rights. And with Marcus hanging around, and all the other trouble in Crookshollow right now, that might make it easier to protect her.

It's a bad idea, Ryan.

I didn't disagree. A well of sadness bubbled up inside me. Suddenly, more than anything, I longed not to be alone anymore.

My head snapped up, the last of my buttons firmly done up, and I met her eyes. She turned her head away, but in that instant, I'd seen something else flicker in her eyes – a mirror of what I felt. Alex Kline was lonely, too. And she was scared.

She needed me. And even though the idea of finding my mate terrified me, I wasn't going to let this remarkable woman sit around being afraid, not when she didn't have to be.

I sauntered over to her, smoothing down my cuffs as I closed the gap between us. As I neared her, the connection tugged at me, pulling us together. She glided forward, as though she were floating.

She held out her hand, the fingers long and beautiful, the palm open, beckoning. Even though my mind screamed at me to ignore the gesture, I took it.

As soon as our fingers grazed, a sliver sliced through my body that had nothing to do with the crisp night air. Her fingers knitted into mine, the perfect fit, like two puzzle pieces slotting into place. I held her hand up in the moonlight and squeezed, my body flooded with radiant energy. Alex's eyes flew open in surprise.

"Wha—what's happening?" she cried.

"I'll explain it all, inside, over a cup of tea." I didn't let go of her hand. I couldn't have, even if I wanted to, which I certainly didn't. Now that I had confirmed the connection, I knew it was all over. I was lost. Alex had me, and I would do anything to keep her safe.

So much for being better off alone.

I tried to smile at Alex, to show her it was okay, but I felt nervous, giddy, like I was a teenage boy on my first date all over again. I opened my mouth to say something witty, but no sound came out.

I'd found my mate, and she was in terrible danger. It was up to me to protect her. But I'd barely held my own life together these past ten years; how could I protect anyone else?

8

ALEX

Ryan's hand in mine pulsed with energy. A strange, tingling sensation ran down my arm, right to my core. It was as if I'd stuck my arm into an electrical socket. What was *that* about? It couldn't be normal. Maybe I was in shock. I'd have to ask Kylie when we got back to the flat.

The flat. Ryan Raynard was coming to my flat. England's greatest artist was going to sit on the couch I'd pulled off the side of the road.

I glanced up at him, just to make sure he was real, totally not to check out his high cheekbones and strong jaw. Definitely not to notice the way his shirt pulled across those muscled shoulders. Why did he have to be so damn hot? Why did he have to be ...

... a shapeshifter.

Just thinking that word made my brain feel like butter. Yep, I was definitely in shock or something. This feeling couldn't be normal. And it would explain why I thought I saw Ryan transform from a fox. There would be some logical explanation that would make perfect sense to me after a cup of tea.

Or maybe something a bit stronger.

Ryan led me back down the street and into the flat, then shut the door and bolted it.

"Alex, what's going on?"

Fuck. I'd forgotten about Kylie. She was sitting on the couch in the middle of the trashed room, stroking a purring Miss Havisham and holding Edgar's black jeans in front of her like they were filled with bees. Furniture lay overturned on all sides. My print of Picasso's *Dora Maar au Chat* had fallen from the wall, the frame broken in three places and glass shards everywhere. The curtains had been torn to shreds and stuffing poured from the couch from what looked like giant claw marks. I peeked around the corner into the kitchen and saw the floor littered with broken china.

Our flat was completely trashed. Despite the strange liquid sunshine coursing through my veins, my heart sank. It may not have been much, but this place was our *home.* Why did those guys have to do this?

Ryan at least had the decency to look guilty. "I'm so sorry about this. I'll pay to have the place cleaned up, don't worry about that."

I glanced at him in surprise. He sounded so different from the cold misogynist I'd met earlier today.

Kylie ignored him. "What's going on, Alex? Why is all our stuff trashed? Why is your hand bleeding? Who is that man?"

Ryan shook his head at me, but I wasn't ready to do him any favours. "Kylie, meet Ryan Raynard, the world-famous artist and arrogant prick I told you about."

"Alex, please," Ryan begged. "You can't just tell her this. We have to be careful to keep it secret—"

I continued, raising my voice to speak over Ryan. I tried to drop his hand, but found it oddly difficult to do. My fingers refused to cooperate. Instead, I shot him a filthy look. Damn him if he was going to come into my house and tell me what to do. "It turns out, in addition to being an arrogant prick, Ryan also transforms into an enormous fox and jumps through people's windows to terrify them half to death. For all I know, he's probably responsible for all those fox attacks in the forest. As to what's going on, he's just about to explain, aren't you, Ryan?"

Ryan sighed. "It's going to sound crazy, but after an introduction like that ... perhaps it won't. Alex, you should sit down with your friend here. Do you need a drink? Tea? Alcohol?"

"No, I do not need a drink. I need you to tell me—"

"G&T, please."

Trust Kylie to forget about the current situation at the mention of a glass of plonk.

Ryan dropped my hand – the sensation like one of great loss – and went to the upcycled tea tray we used as a liquor shelf. Miraculously, it had survived the evening's activities. He found the gin and a bottle of tonic in the fridge. After pouring two G&Ts, he picked up several bottles and shook them, frowning at the labels. "Don't you have any single malt?"

"On our wages?" I scoffed. "We're lucky we can afford gin."

"There's some scrumpy in the fridge, if you're into that," Kylie piped up, standing up and moving into the kitchen. "All Alex's artist friends drink it."

Ryan screwed up his nose, and set about mixing a third gin and tonic. Kylie returned with the first aid kit from the kitchen drawer.

"You've got a nasty cut on your hand," she said, reaching for the hand Ryan had been holding. I could still feel the impression of his fingers, warm and strong against my skin.

"Never mind that," I snapped, not wanting Kylie to touch it and stop the wonderful sensation. "Ryan was going to give us an explanation about the strange people in our house, the raven and the foxes, and the naked man in the street."

Kylie sat up straight, knocking Miss Havisham from her lap. "Who was naked?"

Ryan handed us each a drink, and gestured for me to sit down next to Kylie. My body longed to sit next to him, to touch him again, even if it was just our legs brushing together, but he most inconveniently settled into the single chair opposite us.

I had to squeeze up near the arm of the couch, because Miss Havisham had sprawled out across the centre of the cushions, taking up three-quarters of the space. She opened one lazy eye at me, and began to purr. Ryan shot her a strange glance and took a sip of his beverage.

"You've got your drink," I said. "Now, tell me why there are men's clothes in our living room."

Ryan gestured to Kylie. "You, what's your name?"

"Kylie."

"A pleasure to meet you, Kylie. Now, before I go any further, understand that Alex has ended up mixed up in something pretty dangerous. It's not her fault, and I'm here to see if I can get her out of it. But by telling you what I'm about to tell her, I'm automatically bringing you in as well, and I won't do that without warning you first. Are you prepared to learn something that's going to change your life forever?"

"Of course."

"Can I trust you not to blab this all over the village?"

She nodded, sipping her drink. I scowled at Ryan. "Kylie must know what I know, or I'm calling the police, right now."

He sighed heavily.

"Those clothes are here because when Edgar shifted into his raven form, his clothes don't fit anymore, so they get left behind. Clothes don't shift with the body. Usually, we will hide clothes nearby or shift in our own homes so we don't leave a trail of Calvin Kleins everywhere we go, but when you hit Edgar with that sword, you caught him by surprise. He needed to escape, and that meant a drastic, unplanned shift."

Kylie's eyes bugged out. "What do you mean, shifted? You mean, he turned into a raven?"

"That's exactly what I mean. There are certain humans born

with two forms. They can transform between these forms. Edgar is a bran – a raven shapeshifter. I am a vulpine, and my animal is the fox."

"See, I was afraid you'd say something like that." Hearing him confirm what I'd seen felt surreal. "So this Edgar *shifted* into a raven?"

Ryan nodded. His expressive eyes showed a tinge of ... *something* ... beneath their arrogance. Was it concern for Kylie and I? I didn't want to believe it. "You saw it with your own eyes, Alex, so I don't have to explain to you that it's possible. Shapeshifters ... the kind you've read about in horror stories ... are real. There are many different types of shifters – most shift from human to animal form and back, but there are a few species that shift from animal to animal."

"So the red fox that came through the window and rescued me ..."

"That was me."

"Jesus." Kylie covered her mouth with her hand.

I looked at Ryan, really looked at him, taking in the muscles bulging from beneath his tailored shirt, the way his rust-coloured hair curled around his face, the ends darker, almost tinged with black. His eyes were large, piercing – the eyes of a hunter. I thought of the way he'd had that package of clothes hidden in the bushes. He was cunning and clever, just like the foxes in fairytales.

And his art. Foxes appeared frequently in Ryan's paintings. The critics wrote extensively about their presence – especially the so-called Fox Woman spirit who appeared in the majority of his pieces – identifying them as totems, as woodland spirits, or symbols of British aristocracy. They often pointed to elements of Ryan's paintings that "weren't quite what they seemed."

The truth of Ryan's real life was written into his art, for anyone to read and understand, if they just looked close enough.

If they just saw him transform from a fox into a hot naked man.

Which, I had done. And even though his story was completely crazy and more than a little bit terrifying, I believed him.

At least, I think I did.

"Okay," I said, taking a steadying sip of my G&T. "Okay. You're a shapeshifter. Let's say for argument's sake that this is true."

"It is true."

"I have questions. Do you change into any other animals? Or just a fox?"

"Just a fox. I'm not some kind of sorcerer who can conjure up a new shape whenever I feel like it. Shapeshifting is a genetic trait passed on through generations. In fox-shifters, the gene is dominant in the male line, but in other shifter species, the genetics can be quite different. I've spent years researching shifter mythology, and it seems that practically every ancient civilisation has legends about humans shifting into animals. There are even cave paintings of half-human, half-bear creatures. Human shifters have lived at the edges of civilised society for tens of thousands of years, although mostly in secret—"

"So that other guy was a fox shifter, too," I said, trying to pull him back to the present. I could get a history lesson later.

Ryan nodded. "A few fox clans live near Crookshollow, because the forest is protected, and there aren't as many poachers and hunters as other areas of the country. Vulpines – that's the name for fox shifters – are very territorial. I preside over most of the forest around Crookshollow as part of my family territory. I was out tonight when I smelt that particular fox in my patch. I followed him here. His name is Marcus, and he's a very dangerous vulpine. We've crossed paths before."

"What about the lanky guy with the black hair?" I asked, as Kylie started digging through the first aid kit. "The one who was the raven?"

Ryan gulped down the last of his drink, and poured himself another. "I know him well. Edgar is a hired crook. He's particularly skilled at finding things. Marcus must have requested him especially for this assignment. My guess is, they think you have my paintings. But that's so stupid, because you would have taken the paintings straight to the gallery."

My stomach knotted. Ryan's words only confirmed what the intruders had said. They knew I had the paintings. Kylie glanced at me with wide eyes. I was such a fool, bringing the paintings here. Why did I never, *ever* think these things through? "I can call Matthew immediately and have them moved somewhere more secure—"

Ryan's eyes pierced mine, his expression unreadable. "My paintings *are* here?"

"It's a long story," Kylie said. "If you had Alex's boss, you'd understand."

"You brought ten of *my* paintings to this neighbourhood? Where are they, in the bathtub?"

"In the closet," I said weakly. "In my room. They didn't go upstairs. We've locked them up securely ... I think ..."

"Shit." Ryan shoved his drink into my hand when he saw my worried expression. His fingers brushed mine, sending another surge of energy through me. "I can't believe this. Okay, so the paintings are here. If they knew that, that means they were tracking you from my house. And of course, Marcus would volunteer for this particular mission. You have to be careful, Alex. He's got his eye on you."

"Me?" I took a sip of his drink. Kylie grabbed my other hand – the one that still tingled from his touch – and started to dress the wound.

Ryan nodded. "Because of our connection."

"What connection? We don't have a connection.You don't even like me."

"Don't I?" He smirked as he sipped his drink. Damn, but I wanted to wipe that satisfied smile off his face.

"You need to stop being cryptic, Raynard. Why is this Marcus after me? Does it have to do with my job at the gallery?"

Ryan shook his head. "No, Alex. He's after you because you carry the shifter gene."

9
ALEX

The room fell silent. Ryan's eyes met mine, and as I fell deep into those dark brown pools, my head spun, my mind growing lighter as if it might at any moment float away.

Some invisible energy coursed between us, pulsing in my fingertips from where we'd touched, and swirling around inside of me, calling up strange images in my mind; forgotten memories of my childhood spent roaming in the woods alone, of how the forest called me back, no matter where I was.

It took a few moments for what Ryan said to register, and when it did, it hit me like a freight train.

This can't be real. My fingers clamped around my glass. I didn't know whether I should be knocking it back, or throwing it at Ryan.

"Um ... what?"

"You are related to James Fauntelroy."

Kylie stared at me with interest. "That old official dude your parents named you after. What's he got to do with this?"

Ryan ignored Kylie's question. "What do you know about him?"

I recited the facts like I was in an oral exam, my mind a fog.

"He was a magistrate in the village about two hundred years ago. He brought in all kinds of reforms, including making the forests off-limits to hunters. He was also a defender of witches, and he saved several women from being burned at the stake. There's even a statue of him in the market square."

"Fauntelroy was also a vulpine," said Ryan. "He came from an ancient fox line – the Fauntelroy clan used to dominate this area. That was, until James Fauntelroy fell in love with a human woman – a witch, in fact. They had three children together – all women, and all human. That was the end of the Fauntelroy shifters, but not the end of the Fauntelroy genes."

"I don't understand."

Ryan picked up a legal pad from the mess on the floor, withdrew a pencil from the pocket of his jeans, and scribbled a design. He handed me the sheet of paper, his finger grazing the edge of my hand again. I yanked my hand away as heat sizzled along my palm. "And don't even think about trying to sell that page."

"Why would she do that?" Kylie frowned as she stared at the doodles of foxes and humans, with lines running in all directions across the page. "It's just a sketch of some animals."

"He's Ryan *Raynard*," I said, without thinking. Ryan gave me a searching look, but I ignored it. I wasn't about to launch into an adulating speech on his career in front of him.

"I think I get it," said Kylie, peering over my shoulder. "This is simple, high school biology – Punnett squares and all that."

Ryan nodded. "The gene for shifting is dominant, passed down along the Y chromosome. This means that vulpines are usually always males, although there are some anomalies that have produced female shifters. But mating females – whom we call vixens – carry a unique gene of their own. Only the mating of a vulpine and a vixen will produce shifting offspring. If a vulpine mates with an ordinary, everyday female, like you," he nodded at Kylie, his tone implying she was little more than a bug, "any male offspring they have will most likely become completely human, or they may end up with a strange genetic makeup, a kind of half-shifter state, where they are neither completely human, nor completely fox. We call these anomalies mutts. Marcus is a mutt with some of the worst disabilities I've ever seen in a shifter, which makes him extremely dangerous. He's one of the shifters who has been attacking humans, biting people. I'm sure of it."

Kylie held her hand over her mouth, her eyes wide with fear. "Oh, my god."

"And you're saying I'm one of these vixens?" My temple was starting to throb. "How did I not know about this?"

Ryan nodded. "Even though James Fauntelroy never produced a son, two of his daughters carried his shifter genes, making them highly desirable vixens. And that gene has been passed from generation to generation of Fauntelroy women – until it came to you. When you come of age, the gene caused you to secrete a unique scent, invisible to other creatures, but powerful to the vulpine. When I stepped into the room, Alex, your scent hit me, and from that moment, we were linked."

"Excuse me?" This was just getting more and more intense.

"We are linked, fated to be together," he repeated, his eyes boring into me. "There's a powerful and primal connection between a vulpine and his vixen, Alex, a way to genetically sense the most compatible mate. And, as soon as you entered my property, placed yourself before me, and declared you weren't taken by another, we were bound together. You are destined to be my mate."

"This is ridiculous," I snapped, standing up and walking to the window. I peered out into the night, hoping I wouldn't see the cool grey eyes of Marcus lurking in the darkness beyond. "You can't just decide I'm going to be your ... your mate. I've got my own life, and my own plans, and they don't include being a breeding vessel for an arrogant shapeshifter."

"You don't have to be so hostile. I'm not exactly thrilled about the situation, either."

I balled my hands into fists. "Just what about me isn't good enough for the great Ryan Raynard?"

"It's not that at all." He looked pained. "There's a reason I stay inside my house and away from the world, Alex. I am part fox, and my emotional dynamic is very different from a human man. I crave solitude. I want to be left alone with my paints and my books. I don't want to interact with other shifters, or with humans. I don't want a mate, I don't want cubs, and I really, really don't want to fall in love."

"Why not?"

"That's none of your business," he growled.

"People are breaking into my house, and you just told me we're soulmates or something. You'd better believe it's my business."

He glanced at Kylie, then back at me. His mouth was set in a hard line, but his eyes begged me not to make him talk about himself. I dismissed him with a wave of my hand, indicating he didn't have to say more. He'd already told me his reasons, through his art.

I knew Ryan's whole career, all of his pieces, by heart. His early works were such a celebration of life and colour, but for a few years, around the time he shut himself away in Raynard Hall, they became dark, violent, tortured, pictorial representations of love lost. Ever since, his paintings had evoked a kind of study of opposites, at once both serene and uneasy. All his pieces focused around a central motif of a black-clad woman with come-hither eyes, ruby lips, and a bushy tail. The Fox Woman. Whoever she was, or whatever she represented, she was never far from his mind.

"Do you have sex with foxes?" Kylie blurted out. "Isn't that, like, bestiality?"

"Kylie!"

"Sorry. I'm just trying to lighten the mood."

Ryan managed a weak smile. "Foxes and vulpines don't inter-act, although we can sometimes get into fights if we enter each other's territories. They don't see us as part of their species, nor do we welcome them to mix with ours. We do, however, share the call with foxes, so we might sometimes aid each other to fight off an attacker or to avoid hunters threatening our mutual territories."

I leaned my forehead against the cool glass of the window. "So, let me get this straight. I'm a vixen. My family has carried this fox-mating gene for generations, and now I'm meant to mate with you, and this Marcus is after me ... why?"

"Marcus is obsessed finding a powerful vixen for a mate. It's the only way he can redeem his line from his current mutt genetics. As soon as I made the connection with you, the call revealed you to Marcus, too. He knows you're a Fauntelroy, and he'll stop at nothing to possess you."

"Possess me?"

Kylie threw up her hands. "Jesus, Alex. Marcus wants to have wild shifter sex with you, so you'll give him lots of fox babies."

My skin crawled. The idea that the sandy-haired freak who'd just broken into my house had designs on my body and my womb was more than I could take. "That's barbaric."

"I won't let it happen," Ryan's eyes narrowed. "As your mate, I will protect you."

"I'm *not* your mate. Does what I want have nothing to do with any of this?"

"Fate doesn't take no for an answer. Once I've marked you and our connection is solidified, the only thing that will break it is for him to kill me, and take you for his own. We aren't marked yet, so we're still both able to walk away, but it makes you more vulnerable."

"Marked?"

"A male vulpine will usually mark his female with a bite to claim her as his own."

"I can't believe I'm hearing this."

"It would be safer if you let me do it right now, but I know better than to mark a girl on the first date." He smiled sardonically.

Oh, how that smile turned my insides about. I should've slapped this guy across the face, but instead, a warmth spread through my body, fighting with the fear swirling in my gut. I snapped back a retort, before Ryan could notice that he'd gotten to me. "Especially after you practically fell over yourself trying to escape my presence."

Ryan shrugged. "Now you understand why, so let us forget about that and focus on the task at hand, which is protecting you from another attack by Marcus or one of the other shifters he's allied with. He may be a mutt, but he's powerful, and he has resources, so we can't underestimate him."

"He mentioned someone called Isengrim," I said. "Does that name sound familiar?"

A dark cloud fell over Ryan's face. "Unfortunately, yes."

"Who is he?"

"Another shifter you absolutely don't want to mess with." Ryan glanced at his empty glass, and managed a flicker of a smile. "Also, a story for another night."

"What do we do?" asked Kylie, hugging her knees to her chest, her face drawn with worry. My own chest was tight with fear, as well.

"If you won't let me mark you—"

"Absolutely not." I folded my arms.

"Then, that makes life a little harder, but I can still protect you both," Ryan said. "Even that ridiculous cat. But you have to trust me. You can't go running around with medieval broadswords taking matters into your own hands. I know this world, and we have to do things my way."

I have to be in charge because I'm Ryan Raynard and I don't take orders from anybody, I thought, but didn't say.

I didn't like this. I barely knew Ryan, and he was asking me to trust him? I was used to looking out for myself, and I hadn't trusted anyone in a long time, not since my parents were taken from me. I'd trusted them to always be there, and now they weren't.

Maybe some girls liked a man to come swooping in and save the day, but I wasn't one of them. I was also not the kind of girl who believed in fate or love at first sight, or who thought that some arrogant billionaire artist shapeshifter coming into my home at night and professing we were destined to be together was in any way romantic. The whole situation made me feel queasy.

Except ... I looked at those thick shoulders, and those warm brown eyes, and I wondered what it would be like to be in the care of a man like that. Ryan was so unlike any other man I'd dated. He was so ... unreadable. He intrigued me. I couldn't match his tough, arrogant personality with the delicate, melancholy artwork that gave me an intimate glimpse into the depths of his soul.

Now, knowing what he truly was, I saw his work in a completely new way – the love of the forest landscapes, the intricate relationships between his animals, the way light and shadow played such a pivotal role in his compositions.

I wanted to be inside his head, to see the forest the way he saw it. And, damn me, if I didn't want to press myself against him, to feel the touch of that powerful body, to have his lips devour mine ...

"Are you okay, Alex?" Kylie asked, staring at my face with some concern. "You look all flushed."

I snapped out of my vision, feeling my cheeks grow hot. "I'm fine," I muttered, staring down at my hands, feeling the blush creep down my neck and touch the tips of my ears. "It's just a lot to take in, is all. Can someone refill my drink, please?"

As CONFUSED as I felt around Ryan after everything he'd said, neither Kylie nor I wanted to stay alone in the house. Ryan offered to stay with us. Reluctantly, I accepted.

"There's no spare bed," I said. "And that raven tore up the couch cushions even worse than Miss Havisham, so that's no good, either."

"If you have a few blankets," he suggested, "I could sleep at the foot of your bed. That way, if they try to come in your window, I'll be right there. I'll be in my fox form, of course, so you can sleep soundly knowing your maidenhood is safe."

Kylie chortled, and Ryan cracked a smile at his own joke. I frowned at both of them. That little crack hit too close to home for me. It had been so long since the black metal boyfriend ... so long since someone had loved me ...

Ever since my parents' deaths, I hadn't been able to stomach the idea of having a boyfriend. A couple of guys had asked me out, but I always refused. The idea of loving someone again, when they could just be ripped away from me without warning, turned my stomach.

But being back home in Crookshollow and single made me feel like I'd failed in the real world, and it made me keenly aware of all the reasons I'd left in the first place. The close-minded people who thought art was a waste of time, the subtle jabs from well-meaning friends that my biological clock was ticking away, the sense that I'd reached the last outpost on earth and there was nowhere to go now but off the edge into nothing.

Maybe that's why you keep looking at Ryan like he has potential? Maybe that's why you don't feel as skeeved out by his "fated mates" story as you otherwise would? Because secretly, you want it to be true?

You want the sexy, mysterious artist to sweep you off your feet and take you back to his castle ...

No. I had to stay focused. Ryan was a shapeshifter, and now some other evil shapeshifter was after me. Nothing was what it seemed anymore, and the last thing I needed to be thinking about was some silly fairytale fantasy about being with my idol. Ryan was looking out for me because he felt responsible, and that was all. He was an artist, a weaver of dream worlds – this fated mates thing was just his way of framing the situation.

"What about me?" asked Kylie, staring at Ryan with round, puppy-dog eyes, as she tugged down the neck of her revealing slip.

"It's Alex they're after," he said sternly, not even meeting her gaze. "Don't worry. I'll stay awake the whole night, and I have excellent hearing. If anyone steps a foot – or a paw – on this property, I will hear them."

Why does that statement make my body ache with something like need?

"Have it your way. Goodnight, Ryan. It was a real pleasure to meet you. Don't let Alex tire you out." Kylie winked at me as she passed me on the stairs, sashaying her hips for Ryan's benefit.

Great. Now I was alone with Ryan Raynard, who was staring at me intently with his beautiful dark brown eyes, a curl of red hair falling over the edge of his face. I could feel my cheeks burning as images of his naked body flashed before my eyes. I'd never be able to forget his body as long as I lived.

"Um ... well ... follow me," I mumbled, heading for the stairs. Miss Havisham bounded up ahead of me. Ryan followed behind, and I resisted the urge to sashay my own hips. I wasn't going to play that game, not when he was going to continue with this crazy notion about us being fated to be together. *No matter how much I might want it.*

I went to the linen cupboard and pulled out all the spare blankets, then dumped them on the floor at the foot of the bed, on top of the pile of clothes I had pulled from the wardrobe. "Go to town with those," I mumbled, trying to avoid looking at him as he tugged off his shirt. I still didn't know how I felt about Ryan being in my room, even if it would be in his fox form.

My eyes fell on the portrait of my parents that hung beside the window. Yearning clenched my already nervous stomach. I wanted so badly to talk to them about all this, to ask their advice. But of course, I was on my own.

Mum would freak if she found out I let a man who transforms into a fox and broke in through my window to fight off another fox, sleep in my room. Which is kind of exactly why I'm letting him sleep there, isn't it?

I went to the bathroom, pulled out my toothbrush, and frantically brushed my teeth, wondering as I did why I was brushing my teeth when I had already done it before I'd gone to bed earlier in the evening. I stared in the mirror, noticing for the first time my hair matted against my face, my skin flushed and sweaty, and a big pillow crease across my forehead. Yep, I was ripe for seduction.

Stop it, Alex. You don't want to be seduced. That's your story and you're sticking to it.

I splashed cold water on my face, brushed my hair, and returned to my bedroom. My heart stopped when I saw Ryan standing in the centre of the room, flipping through one of my art journals, his brow creased in amusement as his eyes flicked across the pages.

I crossed the room and snatched it away, my face burning with shame. "Don't touch those," I snapped.

He looked up at me then, and his face looked different, softer. The arrogance had fled it. "They're quite good," he murmured. "You're quite good."

"These aren't mine." I shoved the journal back into the box under my bed. "I just keep them here for a friend. Don't touch them, Ryan, I'm serious."

He shrugged. "I'm sorry. I was admiring the art on your walls, and I saw a palette and easel in the corner, so I assume you paint. I was arranging my bed and I happened to see the box there. Who is your friend? Does she exhibit locally? I'd love to meet her."

"You're a recluse. You don't want to meet *anybody*. Besides, what makes you so sure it's a her?" I breathed.

He took a step closer, his bare chest gleaming under the harsh light. He stared down at me, his eyes so dark they appeared almost black. When he spoke, his voice was low, soft. "There's a sensuality about the lines that only a woman can create. Even though some of the images are quite jarring – almost painful – to view, all have a sense of striking beauty and fierce, quiet resilience. The woman who drew them is a survivor, and someone I would dearly ..." He stepped closer, placing his hand on my arm, his fingers sending an electric charge through my body. "...love to meet."

I opened my mouth to say something. Part of me knew I should force him away, to tell him to leave my house and never come back. But the part of me that had loved his artwork since my university days, that felt the pull of the forest as much as he did, that craved his touch and his wild eyes ... that part of me wanted him to touch more than just my arm.

"Alex ..." he whispered my name and bent his head closer, his lips opening as they moved toward mine. His fingers gripped my arm tighter, his body tensing, moving in for the kill.

My whole body went rigid. *Is he doing this because he wants me? Or is he doing this because he believes we're meant to be together, that I'm meant to be the mother of his cubs?*

I wrenched my arm away, turning my head so his cheek glanced off my shoulder. "She doesn't talk to strangers," I said, my tone icy, covering the regret I felt. I really, *really* wanted to kiss him, to know what it was like to be with Ryan Raynard. But I couldn't, not when he only wanted me for one purpose.

I was not going to be used.

Ryan turned away, not even having the gall to look embarrassed. He rattled the latch on the wardrobe door. "Is this where you're keeping my paintings?"

"It seemed safe enough at the time. I didn't know I had to protect them from crazed fox shifters and raven people, as well as regular old thieves and thugs ..." But Ryan had already moved on, his eye focused on a small framed photo in the corner by the window. My parents and I, when I was a girl, on the broadway.

"Your parents?" He pointed to the people in the picture.

I nodded. "They're both dead. They were killed in a hit-and-run five years ago."

"I'm sorry, Alex."

I shrugged. "Yeah ... so am I. I miss them like hell."

Ryan studied my face, his eyes searching, his expression unreadable. I held his gaze, trying not to let him see how much their loss still affected me. I folded my arms, hiding my trembling hands in my armpits. Ryan's gaze shifted to something over my shoulder, and a thin smile drew across his face.

I spun around, my heart racing as I realised what had caught his eye – the artwork that hung above my bed. A Ryan Raynard print, an early piece pre-Fox Woman period titled *Cunning*. It was not one of his most famous works, but it was the one that spoke to me the most.

In the image, a rabbit chases a butterfly around a grove. A red fox waits in the shadows, its face glued on the rabbit. Its paws are poised, ready to strike, but still it waits, until the rabbit is practically in its grasp. Ryan's brush strokes created a tension in the scene, drawing you into the battle within the fox's mind, poised between the instinct to pounce, and the desire to wait for the bigger payoff.

But, of course, I didn't say any of that. "I like that painting," I mumbled. "Sorry, I couldn't afford the original."

Ryan Raynard stood shirtless in the middle of my bedroom,

and he'd just figured out that I was a fan of his work, and I couldn't say anything that made me sound even remotely intelligent? So much for his fated mate.

"A billionaire fund manager in Tucson bought it from Simon last year," he said quietly. "I actually shed a tear when it left. I think it's one of the finest pieces I've ever done."

"I agree," I said. He stared at me strangely, and I quickly added, "I mean, of your work I've seen. The colour is just so ... good. The way the fox seems to suck in the light as it filters through the leaves, it's almost the opposite of the typical forest scene, where the light streams down on the creature like a spotlight. And it doesn't have the Fox Woman in it. I like that it's different. Why do you paint her, anyway? Is she a real person?"

Ryan's eyes flickered. My chest clenched. Here it was. Here's where he told me that he and the Fox Woman were lovers, that he'd been stringing me along with his crazy story, that I wasn't special at all.

"She's just a character," he said. A dark look passed over his eyes, but it was gone in an instant. "A symbol. She doesn't exist."

I let out a breath I didn't know I was holding. "Oh. Well ... good."

"Good?" He tilted his head to the side.

"No, I mean ... that makes sense. That she's a symbol. You use a lot of symbolism in your work, so ... that's good. What's she a symbol for?"

Ryan paused. "You seem to know an awful lot about my work."

"Not really," I lied, noticing that he hadn't answered the question. "I mean, I had to study up on you for the exhibition. I'm really more into suprematism, and post-painterly abstraction. You know, art that doesn't look so much like stuff."

"Oh yes." Ryan grinned as his gaze circled the impressionist prints hanging from every inch of my walls. "I can see that."

"If you're going to stay in my bedroom, you have to be in your fox form, remember? That was the agreement." I folded my arms across my chest. "Either change now, or get out."

"You could turn away," he growled.

"I want to watch," I insisted. Before, when I saw him shift in the moonlight, I was too shocked to really take in what I was seeing. But now I was able to experience the whole event. I needed to see it again, to convince myself it was true.

Ryan sighed. "Very well." He took a step back from me, undid his fly, sliding his jeans and boxers over his hips and kicking them aside. I now had a completely naked artist in my bedroom. I tried to keep my gaze focused on his face, but it wasn't easy. He stared straight ahead, his eyes unfocused, his hands open, palms facing forward. He took a deep breath, and his body started to change.

It began in his face. His cheekbones protruded, his nose forming a long snout, his lips lengthening, and long canine teeth growing from his mouth. His ears seemed to slide up the sides of his face, and his beautiful rust-coloured hair grew over them. I stared down at his crotch, watching with interest as his pelvis twisted, the bones cracking as they formed an entirely new shape. His genitalia changed so that it resembled that of a dog, and his knees bent in a strange angle as they became hindquarters designed for running and leaping and climbing. A bushy red tail shot out from his tailbone.

Reddish-brown hair grew from the skin on his shoulders and arms, spreading across his body like a strange, quick-growing carpet. Greyish-white hair sprouted on his neck and chest, like the beard of a wizard gone horribly wrong. His body squeezed and contorted, his muscles twitching as they morphed from human to fox. Ryan fell to the ground, landing on his hands, although they weren't hands anymore, but thin, muscled front legs, with five toes containing strong, sharp claws, ready for action.

In less than a minute, Ryan Raynard no longer stood in my

bedroom. Instead, a giant red fox sat on the rug, its head level with my hips. Ryan arched his back and used his back legs to scratch behind his ears. I knelt down beside Ryan, and reached out a tentative hand. He bent his snout forward and nuzzled it, burying my fingers in his soft fur. He pressed his head against my chest, his wet nose nudging my chin. His eyes met mine, and I saw Ryan there, the same intense gaze and lazy arrogance. I scratched behind his ear, and his expression changed to one of complete bliss.

"You know," I said as I scratched harder and his eyes rolled around in his head, his bushy tail twitching back and forth, "I think I like you much better in this form."

He whimpered in protest.

I pointed to the nest of blankets he'd made at the foot of the bed. "To bed with you, Ryan Raynard, before I change my mind about this whole thing."

His tail dragging along the ground, Ryan curled up amongst the blankets, using his snout to push them around to get comfortable. I flicked off the main bedroom light, pulled back my covers, and crawled into bed.

Moonlight streamed over Ryan's back through the bedroom window, and his red fur shimmered, as if it were a bright jewel. He flicked his tail at me, and cocked his head, as if to ask what I was looking at.

I shook my head, laid my head on my pillow, and tried not to think about the man inside the beautiful fox sleeping at the foot of my bed. Feeling happier and more secure than I had in a long time, I turned off my bedside lamp, and fell into a deep sleep.

10

RYAN

lex Kline.

A   I stood beside her bed, my snout resting on the edge of her sheet, and watched her serene face as she slept. I hated myself for standing there like a fool, like a stalker. If she woke up now and saw me, she'd probably kick me out forever.

But I couldn't tear my gaze away.

When I'd seen her room – all the paintings on the walls, the journals filled with scribbled sketches and studies, the shabby secondhand furniture lovingly repainted and repaired, the notes and photographs and ephemera pinned to every surface – I realised I wasn't just talking to a lowly curator, but someone who truly lived for art. Standing amidst all that chaos, all those glimpses into Alex's vivid life, I felt something I hadn't experienced in a long, long time.

I felt a deep sense of comfort.

It was the same feeling that greeted me every time I entered my own studio in Raynard Hall – the sense that anything was possible, that in that space, I could be completely myself. It was the closest thing to the freedom of the forest in the real world.

I knew I'd stepped into Alex's space, her freedom. And that

made me feel both honoured and incredibly determined. Even though she didn't have much choice, she had let me in here. And judging by that painting – my *painting* – hanging over her bed, I thought I could understand why.

Alex let out a snort, and pulled the blanket tighter under her chin. She didn't wake up. Raw energy sizzled between us, the unspoken connection that drew us together.

I already knew that she was headstrong and clever. And more than a little reckless – after all, she was storing my paintings in her closet. Now, staring down at her like this, I could see too that she was vulnerable. I hated that I'd burst into her life like this and caused all this chaos. I'd thought I could just forget her, to carry on as though I'd never established the connection between us and identified her as my mate.

But now ... now I wanted to fight for her.

She was worth fighting for.

11

ALEX

I woke up the next morning to find the fox gone. There was an indentation in the blankets from his body, but he was nowhere to be seen. My stomach clenched in fear. I tugged on the wardrobe door. It was still locked. *Phew.*

I heard Ryan's voice in the kitchen below, and Kylie's laughter floated up the stairs. For some reason, this made me feel jealous. *Why have I been sleeping while she's downstairs eating breakfast with Ryan? Why is she so interested in him, anyway? She's dating Ray the reenactment geek, and she doesn't even know anything about art.*

The thought was so crazy, I slapped my cheek, trying to shock myself back to reality. Kylie wasn't after Ryan. She was my best friend in the world, and she was just a vivacious, friendly person who was having an easier time resolving this whole shapeshifter thing that I was. And I needed to get down to breakfast and see what was going on. Maybe, the harsh light of the morning would shine some light on my jumbled feelings.

I pulled on my best dressing gown (made from red satin, and containing no holes), stopped in the bathroom to gargle and brush down my bed hair, and padded downstairs.

I found Kylie sitting at the kitchen table, retelling one of her favourite anecdotes about the time she was invited to tea at Buckingham Palace and ended up getting completely trashed and breaking her heel on the lawn. Ryan stood in human form in front of the stove, flipping an omelette in the pan and nodding at appropriate moments.

Miss Havisham sat on the corner of the counter, attempting to hook a rasher of bacon from out of the container. I glanced around the room, hardly believing what I saw. Everything had been cleaned up and put back in place, except the smashed painting, which lay in a plastic bag by the front door.

Ryan's face was focused as he expertly flipped the omelette in the pan. He looked even better than I remembered, with his red hair all rumpled, the curls falling over his warm, brown eyes.

"—and then my aunt said we should celebrate with a few pre-tea glasses of champagne, and then—"

"Hey." I waved timidly from the doorframe.

Ryan dropped the spatula against the pan. "Good morning, Alex," he said stiffly, his expression impossible to read.

His reaction sucked the wind out of me. I mean, I didn't expect him to rush over and hug me, but his formality seemed so at odds with the way he was last night, especially when he was being so flirty with Kylie.

Is he upset with me, because I rejected him last night? Is Ryan Raynard upset with me? That was a weird thought.

I gestured around the clean kitchen. "When did you have time to do this?"

"When it became clear the sun was rising and Marcus wasn't coming back. I couldn't abandon my post and fall asleep, so I got up and cleaned up a little."

"Thank you," I said.

He shrugged, avoiding eye contact. "No need to thank me. If it weren't for me, nothing would have needed cleaning up in the first place. I'll buy you another print to replace the one that broke."

"Don't worry about it. I work in an art gallery. They sell those things in the lobby for ten quid," I replied. There was an awkward silence, before I added, "Something smells good."

That got a little smile. Ryan lifted a fresh omelette from the pan, folded it with all the confidence of a celebrity chef, and presented the plate to me.

"I didn't expect Ryan Raynard to know his way around the kitchen." I slumped down opposite Kylie and dug in. The omelette was delicious. "I thought a rich snot like you would have a kitchen staff preparing *foie gras* and snail droppings twenty-four hours a day."

"A man cannot live on snail's droppings alone," Ryan replied in a monotone as he cracked more eggs into the pan. "You're right, though – usually Simon prepares my food. Before I returned to the family manor, I lived in an artist's squat in Belfast for a few years. You learn fast that cooking skills are a commodity that can be bartered for cigarettes or clean blankets. I never stopped enjoying being in the kitchen."

Ryan lived in an artist's squat? There was nothing about that in his official biographies, although they were pretty thin on information. With his expensive shirt and tailored jeans, he didn't look the type.

The more I learned about the man I'd admired for years, the more of a mystery he seemed.

"Well, it paid off, let me tell you. Do you think it's something to do with being a fox? The scents and things?"

Ryan looked up from the pan and met my eyes for the first time, a strange expression on his face. "That's very insightful. I'd never thought about it, but you're probably right."

Kylie smiled at me from across the table as she stuffed the last square of omelette into her mouth. "What are you doing today, Alex?" she asked, her mouth still full of egg.

"I have to take Ryan's paintings to the gallery. They need to go into cataloguing today if we've any hope of getting everything hung in time for the opening. *Someone,"* I shot Ryan a filthy look, "insisted on a ridiculously tight exhibition deadline."

"I'll take you into the gallery," Ryan offered.

I spat out my juice. "Excuse me?"

"I'll drive you to the gallery. Marcus could well try something again, and I still intend to make good on my promise to protect you. Besides, I'm the artist. I should make sure my paintings arrive at the venue in the appropriate condition."

"Ryan, I don't think you understand. There are *people* at the gallery. A lot of art people who will be dying to meet the man who hasn't been outside his manor in ten years. You're going to get swarmed. Are you ready for that?"

"Maybe I am." His smile wavered a bit. "Maybe I'll go in disguise."

"What? Like, with a fake moustache and a fedora? Or, I know, you'll go in your fox form. That's it, I'll just walk a fox inside. What do I tell Callahan? 'Don't worry, sir. The fox is just another part of the exhibition. Raynard is experimenting with naturalism – this fox here is his attempt to place the viewer inside the painting...' No, Ryan, that won't work."

He laughed, his face relaxing. I grinned, realising how much I hated his formal manner.

"You're not thinking clearly, Alex. If I haven't left the house in ten years, no one knows what I look like. They won't realise a thing. Now, where is your car?"

"On the street, why?"

"We'll need to take it. I came here through the forest. I don't have my car. I don't even own a car. Well, I think I do, some sort of expensive English contraption, but Simon is the only one who uses it."

"You don't even know if you own a car?" Kylie exclaimed. "Rich people have very different lives."

"We sure do. So how about it?" Ryan's face lit up like an excited child.

"You want to drive *my* car?" My mind reeled as I thought of all the takeout containers, fashion magazines, dirty laundry and art books strewn across the backseat of my little Fiat.

"Simon never lets me drive his, and it's been too long since I've given it a go. Besides, they're my paintings. I'd feel better knowing I was the one at the wheel should anything happen. It's my responsibility to protect you, too." Ryan picked up his own plate. "I can't do that if I'm not near you."

"Fine," I shovelled in another mouthful of omelette. "Give me twenty minutes to get dressed. And get some coffee brewing. I'm going to need it."

FORTY MINUTES LATER, I gripped the edges of my seat, my knuckles turning white with terror, while Ryan threw my little car around the streets of Crookshollow like he was on a Formula 1 track, oblivious to all known traffic laws. In the boot, ten priceless paintings bounced and slid against each other.

The boot wouldn't even lock now. Marcus had obviously bashed his way in last night, and broken the lock. In the end, we'd had to duct tape it shut. Matthew was going to *kill* me. That was, *if* I survived the drive.

"I haven't been behind the wheel since my days in Belfast." Ryan laughed as he careened around a corner, cutting off a large lorry exiting Prince Edward Drive. I cringed as horns blasted in our wake.

Once on the high street, Ryan weaved in and out of lanes. "Watch out!" I cried as he raced through a traffic light, narrowly missing a woman pushing her pram across the street. I shut my eyes, unable to watch. I heard my brakes squeal, and the women shouted something unseemly though my open window.

"Oops." I opened my eyes to see Ryan smiling at me. Despite the situation, my insides turned all giddy. *Dammit.* I didn't want to like him. He was so ridiculously out of my league, and this whole vulpine / fated mates thing was doing my head in. But the more time I spent with him, the closer I was to falling for him. And that was bad, bad, bad. I wasn't ready to trust anyone again, least of all Ryan Raynard.

"You'd better not think this is funny," I snapped, trying to hide my desire behind scorn. "Park in here." I pointed to a building up ahead.

"Don't you have a space at the gallery?"

I shook my head. I actually did, but it was right next to Matthew's space, and the last thing I wanted was for Ryan to crash my car filled with priceless paintings into my boss' Mercedes. Ryan turned into the building's entrance, scraping my door along the concrete barrier, and miraculously managed to park on the third floor without hitting anyone. I opened the boot and was surprised to see none of the crates were damaged. Ryan picked up the three largest pieces, while I carried a stack of smaller paintings. We descended the fire escape, Ryan leaping the steps three at a time, while I leaned against the wall and slid along the balustrade, feeling out each step with my heels before I set down my foot.

I'm walking down the fire escape, carrying millions of dollars-worth of precious modern art in my hands, and the world's most sought-after art celebrity – who also happens to be a shapeshifter – is walking in front of me, whistling "Eye of the Tiger" under his breath.

Surreal.

At the staff entrance, I swiped my ID card, and walked through a dark hall into the main storage and inventory space. It was early, and, although there were lights on in the offices, the warehouse was still shrouded in darkness. At least Ryan's first daylight foray into the real world wouldn't involve too many direct confrontations with people.

I flicked the lights on, watching the fluorescent tubes flicker to life. "Quickly, in here." I pulled Ryan down the aisle for incoming exhibitions that needed cataloguing. I found the bay we'd set aside for his work, and dumped the seven heavy wooden frames into it.

"With any luck," I whispered to Ryan as he stacked his three frames behind them, "if we hurry, I can get you out of here before anyone sees—"

"James Alexandra Kline!"

I spun around, my heart pounding against my chest. "Matthew, hi." I wiped my hair out of my eyes, certain my face must betray my nervousness. "It's a beautiful morning, isn't it?"

Matthew folded his arms across his wide chest. "Darryl just came up to see me. He said the Raynard paintings still haven't been delivered. I gave you *one* chance, Kline, one big opportunity to make a name for yourself with the exhibition of the year, and you blew it—"

Ryan stepped forward, eyes blazing. I threw an arm out in front of him, shoving myself in front of him. I couldn't predict what Ryan was going to do, but the last thing I needed was Ryan laying into Matthew. But Ryan was too fast. He slipped around my arm and stepped right up to Matthew.

"Darryl needs to get his eyes checked," he growled. I gestured frantically at him to shut up, but if he saw me, he was ignoring me. He pointed at the bay we just finished loading. "All the Raynard paintings are right there."

Matthew's eyes narrowed. "Who are you? Alex, you know you're not allowed unauthorised visitors down in the warehouse."

"Uh ... this is Damian. He's ... uh, an intern from the university," I said hurriedly. "He's going to be helping me with the cataloguing."

"Oh really? Did I authorise a budget for that?"

"He's volunteering," I said meekly.

Matthew shot Ryan a murderous glare. Ryan glared right back, but he did step away. Matthew gave me a pained look, as if he couldn't bear my stupidity a moment longer. He turned away, dismissing me with a wave of his hand. "Whatever, I don't care. Just get these catalogued today so they can be hung tomorrow. If you need me, I'm going to be yelling at Darryl."

"Don't stress your vocal chords too much," I said. "You've got plenty more yelling to do before this thing goes public."

He snorted, shaking his fist at the roof. "Tell me about it. I didn't even want this bloody exhibition in the first place. Raynard is an arrogant shit. He must be running low on cash if he wants this exhibition so badly. But of course, we have to do it on *his* terms. We have to bow down to the great *Almighty Artiste*. Did you meet him yesterday? Is he as big a prick as I imagine?"

Ryan looked ready to throw a punch.

"Oh, no sir," I stifled a giggle. "He's an even bigger prick."

Matthew snorted with amusement, then stormed off, yelling for Darryl.

Ryan turned to me. "I'm hurt," he pouted. "Is that any way to talk about the man who saved your life?"

"That wasn't the man," I replied. "That was the fox. I like the fox, but the man I'm still undecided on."

He grabbed my wrist, pulling me close to him, pressing his broad chest against mine. "What about now?" he growled, his eyes boring into mine. I wondered if he could feel my heart as it quickened against my chest. The tension between us crackled like lightning. I wanted nothing more than to reach up and press my lips to his ...

But I knew it would only end in heartache. Ryan wanted me because he believed I was his fated mate. But that wasn't the way I did things. I needed to *choose* Ryan, and that meant I had to trust him. Right now, I barely knew him, except as the artist I'd admired from afar. I needed to figure out if I liked him for who he was, not for what his work meant to me.

As Ryan leaned forward, his eyes burning with intense desire, I turned my head away, wrenching myself free of his grasp.

He advanced again, and I backed away until my back pressed

against a rack of crates. I held my hands up. "Don't come any closer," I warned. "I can't think straight when you're too close."

Ryan looked confused. "Alex?" he breathed. "What's wrong? Don't you want this? Don't you feel *something* when we're together ..."

I shook my head, forcing myself to ignore the hurt look in his soft eyes. "It's not that I don't feel anything for you," I said. "It's this fate thing. I can't help but feel as if this ... *chemistry* between us is forced upon me, because you're telling yourself that we're meant to be together, and I'm responding to all those foxy pheromones."

Ryan took a step forward. "Why is that a bad thing?"

"If I'm with a man, it needs to be on my own terms. Fate has no place in my life, Ryan." *Because if there's such a thing as fate, that means I was meant to lose my parents, and I want no part of a universe that believes that.* "I want a choice. I *demand* a choice."

Ryan's shoulders sagged, and he glanced down at his shoes. A long, expressive silence flowed between us, broken only by the buzz of the fluorescent lights overhead. When he looked up again, that same self-satisfied smirk was on his lips once more.

"Very well," he said. "You will have a choice, Alex. I just have to get you to choose me."

"That's all I ask."

"Challenge accepted."

I relaxed, feeling the awkward moment had passed. Ryan's eyes were lit up, as if the idea of convincing me to choose him was like some kind of great adventure. That made my stomach dance with joy. "C'mon, Damien," I said, heading for my office and beckoning him to follow. "We need to get these paintings catalogued."

12

RYAN

I was no longer Ryan Raynard. I was now "Damien" the intern, cataloguing priceless paintings (and very good paintings too, if you want my totally inexpert intern's opinion) with the help of the gallery's two young, blonde assistants.

When I say these assistants were "helping," what I really mean was that they were falling over each other to sit next to me, deliver my coffee, and hand me the pen. They broke into high-pitched giggles every time I spoke. I half expected one of them to start shining my shoes.

While the attention was flattering, it got old fast. A man's ego could only do with so much stroking, and I was not used to this much noise and stimulation around me while I focused on a task. Besides, with my eyes flicking through the glass partition to Alex's office across the hall every five minutes, where she was typing on her computer and wearing a pair of dark-rimmed glasses that I knew would now appear in every one of my fantasies, my attention was very definitely elsewhere.

I was so distracted, in fact, that I didn't have much of a chance to focus on the fact this was the longest I'd sat inside a room with strangers for the last ten years, Alex and Kylie excepted. Not just any strangers, either – giggling strangers who were trying to flirt with me.

This whole day had been rather surreal – my first night away from the manor, driving a car for the first time in a decade (when did everyone get so *slow*?), setting foot inside an actual gallery, talking to Alex's boss. I'd done all this without even blinking an eye, barely stopping to take in the strangeness of it all.

In one day of knowing her, this woman had given me more confidence back than I'd managed to carve out for myself in the last decade. With Alex, it all seemed so easy. I was no longer entirely sure why I'd left all this behind in the first place. Being with her made me feel the same way as when I was running through Crookshollow Forest – wild and invincible, like I could do anything.

Maybe I could. Maybe, with Alex by my side, I really could do anything.

With a final round of giggles, I managed to get the girls to finish the last painting. I glanced at my watch. It was just past 11 a.m. I left the two girls to finish the last bit of paperwork, pushed my way out of the office, and knocked on Alex's door. She glanced up, the glasses slipping down the bridge of her gorgeous nose, and waved me in.

"Save me from their incessant prattling," I demanded, shoving the door so hard it banged against the glass behind it.

Alex lifted her glasses off her nose in mock surprise. "You mean you haven't gained any deep intellectual insights from your morning with Trixie McBimbo and Alice Legsakimbo?"

"Conversational stimulation is clearly not their forte." I leaned across the corner of her desk, pushing my face as close to hers as I dared. *Do the glasses thing again, Alex.* My cock was already straining against my jeans. I breathed in deep, and her spicy, intoxicating scent coursed through my whole body. "You can have a break now, right? I want to walk through the museum."

Alex glanced down at her computer. I noticed a hundred post-it notes stuck around the outside of the screen, obscuring the edges of the spreadsheet she had open. She wrung her hands, biting her lower lip. *Damn, when she combined that with the glasses ...*

"I have so much work ..." Her voice trailed off.

"What is work for, if not to be put off until the very last minute? Come on, I want to see where my paintings will hang. You can't deny me – I'm the artist."

Alex pursed her lips. My whole body itched to lean forward and press my lips against her, to experience the joy of her flesh. The energy between us tugged me closer, closer ...

But I couldn't. I'd promised her I would let her choose. If I wanted to win her, I had to do it the old-fashioned way, no matter how much my cock screamed otherwise. At least I knew the way to Alex's heart was through art.

I snapped my body back, and slapped the corner of her desk. "Alex, let's go."

"Ryan, it's a public gallery. Are you sure you're ready for that?"

I paused. I'd been so distracted by her, I hadn't even thought about the people milling around in the office. Alex fitted so well into this world, I kind of slotted in alongside her, as though I'd been around people my whole life, no worries.

But going downstairs was different. Being in the offices was one thing, but out there anyone could spot me, recognise me. There had been a few tabloid pictures of me released over the years, taken over the wall with long scopes while I'd spoken to stonemasons or walked to the edge of the forest. Out in the public galleries were actual art critics and collectors, people who would know what I looked like, even after ten years.

The thought of being recognised, of having cameras shoved in my face and people demanding more of me than I had to give turned my stomach. But if I wanted Alex, I was going to have to get over it. Besides, she had so much to teach me.

She tilted her head to the side. "Ryan, you okay?"

"Yes," I said firmly, extending a hand out to her. "In fact, I insist. I haven't been outside the manor in so long, Alex, except to hunt in the woods. I didn't realise how much I'd missed it, until today. I want to see artwork hanging on walls, not in books or on a computer screen. But most of all, I want to see them with you."

An adorable flush coloured her cheeks. She glanced down at her phone. "I can take two hours, since my cataloguing team seems to work twice as fast with you around—"

"I crack the whip," I smirked.

"I guess ... I'll need to work late tonight anyway. There's still a lot to do to prepare your exhibition. But sure, I can take you through the public galleries." She tossed her phone down on her desk. "*If y*ou promise not to draw attention to yourself."

"I can't help where people's eyes wander, but I'll do my best."

Alex stood up, and placed her hand uncertainly in mine. A blast of energy surged down my arm. She must've felt it too, because she jerked her hand away.

"Don't worry." I held out my hand again. "It's the connection between us. It tries to pull us together, like a magnetic field. I can ignore it, if you can."

I couldn't ignore it, but she didn't need to know that.

Alex frowned, but placed her hand in mine again. My whole arm tingled. Her soft fingers against mine fitted together perfectly. She didn't pull away. She glanced up at me, her face breaking out into a smile that melted my heart.

Ignoring the jealous glare of the assistants from across the hall, Alex and I walked through the staff lounge and out into the gallery itself. She took me straight to the west hall, where my work would be displayed.

Currently, the space was filled with a kinetic exhibit; a large section of the room had been given over to a garden of multi-coloured paper windmills glued to a fibreboard floor. Fans disguised in towering white mushroom-like sculptures blew the windmills this way and that. From the ceiling hung an enormous mobile – a neo-objectivist study in the style of early Rodchenko, Alex informed me – of interconnected swirls and whirring gears made from hammered tin and wood. On the far wall, a metal ball rolled around in a strange, malleable corrugated maze, making a disharmonious gurgle as it rolled over the metal ripples. A plaque in front of the display invited the viewer to move the ball or change the course of the maze.

I stood in front of this piece for a long time, watching the ball roll back and forth. When I first started visiting art galleries as a boy, I never saw this type of art in fancy, airy spaces like Halt – it was always relegated to small, dimly-lit independent spaces run by artist collectives and eccentric billionaires. My fingers itched to push the ball and interact with the piece, the way you were supposed to, but I held back. Alex's warm fingers in mine rooted me in place.

As we stood there in silence, two young boys shoved in front of us and started pushing the maze around, creating new shapes.

I smiled. "This is a fun piece. But it's not art as I know it. I don't look at this and see into the artist's soul. I don't feel as if I've stepped into a world out of my being. I just feel entertained by the moving ball and that strange, otherworldly sound."

"It's a statement about the world," Alex said. "Kinetic art is all about bringing the audience inside the piece itself, to show that each person is part of the problem, and part of the solution. This art is never static, it is created in the moment – right now, as those boys are playing, they are part of the work itself."

"I see," I replied. "Do you like this kind of stuff?"

"I think it's a great way to get the public in the door," Alex said. "The first exhibit I curated at the Tate was a kinetic show, and it had a record turnout. Once people come in the door, they start to engage with the other, less hip work. But no, it's not the kind of art that moves me. I'm a bit more ..." She looked away. "Traditional, I guess."

I remembered the prints on her walls, all from artists that also adorn my home gallery. And above her bed, pride of place, was my *Vixen*. Did *my* art move her? Thus far, Alex has been very cryptic when I asked her about my art. Usually, I paid no care to what anyone thought of my work, but the idea that she saw something in my pieces ... my chest clenched tight, and I found my next breath a struggle.

For the next two hours, we walked hand in hand, looking and commenting on the paintings and sculptures on display. I dragged Alex from piece to piece, scrutinising every detail and leaning on her for commentary on the work, the artist, the treatment of materials. We could have been any couple visiting the gallery, not the self-conscious gallery curator and the reclusive celebrity artist who turns into a fox.

I had a deep knowledge of the art world, having lived and breathed art since I could first hold a brush. But my exposure to modern art stopped when I became a recluse. With my fancy public-school education, I knew much of the Renaissance, the Impressionists, the Pre-Raphaelites ... all the members of the old boy's club. Through Simon's diligent efforts, I'd managed to acquire some remarkable pieces for my own collection.

But in my isolation, I hadn't been able to gorge myself on fresh ideas from the art world. My gallery was exactly the same every time I visited it. I hadn't realised, until I beheld the Halt's exhibits, just how out of touch I was. There was so much to discover. The Halt Institute had an exhibition on Fauvism that engaged me for more than thirty minutes. I painstakingly examined of every inch of the small canvases, drowning in the bold colours of the French "wild beasts."

A photographic exhibition of political street art from the Middle East left me baffled, as did a video projection of two men blowing red-coloured bubbles into each other's mouths through a pink straw, interspersed with extreme panning close-ups of a cactus.

"To be honest, I didn't really get that one, either," said Alex.

"I can't believe some of this stuff," I said, walking with her through a small hallway filled with abstract Botswannian folk art.

"How do you survive as an artist when you don't even know what's big in the art world, or what the galleries and collectors are looking for?" she asked.

"Simon takes care of selling my paintings and all the other business details for me. All I do is paint, read books, and hunt in the forest. It's very freeing. I don't have a thousand contemporaries swimming around in my head. I'm not really part of a movement, or a school."

"Yes, you are. You're a Neo-Impressionist. *The* Neo-Impressionist, depending who you talk to."

I wondered if that was her opinion, but I didn't want to embarrass her by asking. Instead, I shrugged. "Maybe, but I couldn't name any of the other Neo-Impressionists. I don't know their work, as they know mine. I don't see what they're doing, I just see my own work. When I want inspiration, I head into the woods. As such, my work does not look like anyone else's, because no one else is like me."

We paused in the door of the main gallery, where the sign pointed to a permanent exhibition of works from the greatest painters of the last five hundred years. My gaze swept immediately to the Picasso on the far wall.

My whole body stiffened. My mouth dried out. I floated across the room, the painting drawing me in with a magnetic force almost as powerful as the one holding me to Alex. The gallery disappeared – the laughing children, the *clop-clop-clop* of high heels on the hardwood floors, the steady *pop* of bubbles from the projection room.

I'd seen a Picasso only once before, in a Belfast gallery shortly after I left London. My reaction had been similar then; a deep, visceral tugging, as though my whole body longed to topple inside the painting and exist within that monochrome world of angles and corners.

"... Ryan? ... Are you okay?" A hand waved in front of my face. Alex sounded concerned.

I opened my mouth to answer her, but no sound came out. I tried to tear my eyes away, but found the task impossible. I was lost, utterly entranced. The lines leapt across my vision, and I could *see* what this great man was thinking, how he moved through the world in a completely new way. His brush formed the beauty he saw in everyday objects – how a simple kettle and bowl of fruit became a complex map of lines and shapes. How he used bold lines to draw the eye to the spaces in between, the shapes that were beauty personified.

When I fell into that painting, I discerned the construction of the universe, the beauty of the world on an atomic level. Tears formed in the corners of my eyes. I didn't dare blink, not wanting to break the spell of the painting. The tears spilled down my cheeks.

"Ryan?"

Alex. Panic seized me. I didn't want her to see me like this. I stepped back, shaking my head, the spell broken.

"Ryan, you're crying."

I rubbed my eyes. "Yeah, allergies."

"You're allergic to Picasso?" Alex tilted her head to the side, pushing her glasses up her nose. Damn, Picasso should have painted those glasses; it might've been the most erotic image in his *oeuvre*.

I finished wiping my eyes with the back of my hand. "It's so stupid. Only once before have I seen a Picasso in the flesh, and I reacted exactly the same way. I've seen them in books, of course. I have thousands of art books in my house, but it's not the same. I've had Simon search for one for my private collection, but they're impossible to get on the black market unless you're a

Saudi royal or an American rockstar. I never thought to see one for real again. The lines, Alex! It's just amazing."

"I know," she whispered back, squeezing my hand. "The first time I came to this gallery, it stole my attention. The way he uses shape to convey every side of an object, as if he's reaching back in time and forward into the future at once. Sometimes I come here to eat my lunch, and I just sit and stare at it, wondering about the mind behind such a work."

"Don't tell anyone that I ..." I pointed to my eye.

She laughed. "You mean that you got a piece of dust in your eye? No, Ryan, I won't ruin your street cred, as long as you don't tell Matthew I eat in the gallery."

"Deal." I held up her hand, and clasped it between both of mine. The heat of her touch radiated through my arm, lighting a torch deep within my chest. "Thank you, Alex. Thank you for this."

"You're welcome." Her eyes bore into mine, deep pools of brown, like the tones of a Picasso.

I stepped forward, my gaze lowering to her lips. They called to me, begging for my touch. I stepped forward again, closing the space between us. Only our clasped hands prevented our bodies from being pressed against each other.

"Ryan—" she breathed.

I bent down. My eyes locked with hers. Heat surged through my body, pulling me closer, like a moth to a totally irresistible flame. Her scent enveloped me, sending a shiver of delight right through my chest. I leaned forward, and brushed my lips against hers. Fire flared in my veins as her soft lips slid open around mine.

My tongue sought hers, deepening the kiss. My arms itched to be around her, to mash her body against mine and relieve the tension floating in the air between us. But I didn't dare drop her hand. I couldn't bear severing the connection.

The heat of her lips lit a path straight to my cock, which

throbbed urgently against my jeans. *My mate. I've found you at last—*

"James Alexandra Kline," a voice thundered over the loudspeaker. Alex leapt from my arms, her face white as a sheet.

No. This can't be happening.

"Attention, James Kline, please make your way to the boardroom immediately."

Alex's eyes darted all around the room, looking everywhere but at me. "I ... I have to go."

Her heat still tingled on my lips. "Alex, don't leave like this—"

"I *can't,* Ryan. This was a mistake. I shouldn't even have been down here. There's *so much* work to be done. And I'm ... I'm ..." She threw up her hands.

"I'll go. I'll leave you alone. Just promise me you're not running away."

"What about Marcus?"

"He's hardly going to come in here with all these people about. I'll be back at 7 p.m. to pick you up. Give me your keys and I'll get out of your way."

She backed away, shaking her head. "I'm not giving you my car."

"Why not?"

"Do you even have to ask?"

I set my mouth into a firm line. "Fine. I have other ways of getting around."

"Ryan Raynard." Her voice was ferocious. "If you shift into a fox within the walls of this gallery, I will *never* forgive you. What are you going to do?"

"I'm going to walk around a bit, explore Crookshollow in the daylight, feel the pavement beneath my feet." I smiled, touching my finger to my lips. "I've got a taste for the real world again."

Alex made a strangled sound in her throat. "I *really* have to go."

"Fine, go back to your Matthew. But don't forget I'll be here at seven for dinner. Perhaps I'll hunt us out a good restaurant."

"I'd like that." She smiled, the sight of it catching my chest in a vice. Before I could say another word, she whirled around and darted away, leaving me with only the trail of her scent and the fire of her lips on mine to sustain me until dinner.

ALEX

H e kissed me. *Ryan Raynard just kissed me in front of a Picasso.*
I floated up the stairs to the offices in a daze, the heat
of his touch still tingling against my lips. I could still feel the
ghost of his fingers against my hand.

Matthew was at the top of the stairs waiting for me, and his
face was stony. He launched into one of his rants. I nodded and
frowned, but I didn't hear a word he said. I kept replaying the kiss
over and over and over, reliving every glorious moment of it.

I'd never had a kiss that felt like that before, like I'd plugged
my lips into an electrical socket, like I was a Tesla coil charged
with lightning.

There was so much that needed to get done in order to have
the exhibition ready for the opening in two weeks. I tried to force
Ryan out of my head and focus on my work, but it was practically
impossible. I had to give the assistant's instructions three times
because I forgot what I was saying, and I asked Tara to forward
me the same email three times. Matthew yelled at me twice more,
but I couldn't even say why.

Every time I saw Ryan's name printed on a file or a brochure,
my whole body surged with heat.

At 4 p.m., we closed the west gallery, and I supervised the installation team as they packed down the kinetic exhibit in preparation for hanging Ryan's paintings. It was no easy feat. The exhibition was moving on to a London gallery, which meant that *every single* windmill had to be individually wrapped in tissue paper and packaged so as not to bend or squash them. I had taken my laptop in with the intention of catching up on emails while I supervised, but when it became clear we weren't going to be able to leave until midnight, I grabbed some paper and tape and joined the fray.

I wanted to cry. I had no way of reaching Ryan to tell him I'd be late. I couldn't even go out into the parking lot at seven to try and catch him, as Matthew was also working late and the way he glared at me strongly implied that if I so much as went to the bathroom before the job was done, I'd be out in my arse.

I managed to sneak out at 7:45 after begging for a bathroom break. Ryan was nowhere to be seen. Even though I expected it, that dark, empty parking lot sank my stomach down to my knees.

We didn't finish packaging flowers until nearly 10 p.m. My rumpled dress clung to my sweat-soaked body. My hair was a mess of frizzy strands sticking out from my ponytail. My eyes were ringed with dark circles, and my muscles ached as though I'd just ran a marathon (not that I'd ever run a marathon, so I suppose it wasn't a fair comparison, but I was extrapolating based on the most painful experience I could possibly conceive of).

So much for my date with Ryan. Disappointment surged through me as I gathered my things and turned out the lights in the office.

I swiped my way out of the door, and stopped to clip my card on to the strap of my purse.

"Fancy meeting you here."

I whirled around. Ryan was leaning nonchalantly against a pillar which only a moment ago had been completely devoid of his presence. He'd changed his clothes, and now wore an exquisite pair of black jeans and a leather jacket. A pair of designer sunglasses perched on his head.

"You look ..." I struggled to find the words. He looked smoking hot, more like a rockstar than a famous artist.

He gave me a brilliant smile. "I decided if I was going to take the brilliant Alex Kline out for dinner, I should look worthy of her company."

I blushed. "I can't believe you still want to take me out. It's so late. Have you been waiting all this time?"

"Not that long." He jabbed a finger at the glass wall of the gallery. "One advantage of working in a fishbowl is that it's easy for potential dates to glance inside and see that you're still occupied."

"I'm sorry. Things took way longer than they were meant to. I never want to see another paper pinwheel for as long as I live. I look awful, and you look—" The word *gorgeous* died on my lips.

"I think you look just fine," he growled, his eyes flicking down my body in a way that made me ache all over, and not from exhaustion.

"Do we still have a booking? Everything's probably closed by now." My chest was swelling as he grabbed my hand and started pulling me toward the street.

"Not this place," was his reply. A cab waited at the kerb, the engine idling. Ryan held the door of the cab open for me.

"What? No limo?" I joked. "In the movies, billionaires always drive around in limousines."

"A limo seemed awfully tacky," he replied. "I won't stay rich if I spend all my money on frivolous indulgences."

"What about your car, the one Simon uses?"

"He needed it. He has his salsa class tonight. I *can* take a cab, you know. You're talking to a guy who used to slum it in Belfast, remember?" He closed the door and then leaned in through the open window, not wanting to be apart from me any more than I wanted him to leave my side.

"With all due respect, there's slumming it, and then there's *slumming it*. Actual poverty versus what spoiled rich kids do when they've read too much Hunter S. Thompson and want to be rebellious." I settled myself into the seat. "That leather jacket must have cost a pretty penny, Mr. Slumming It."

"And I don't regret a single cent," he replied, as he bent down and kissed me.

The kiss shocked me, but as soon as his lips were against mine, I was completely under his spell. I opened my lips and Ryan slipped his tongue against mine, deepening the kiss. He lifted his hands to my cheeks, pulling my face against his, forcing himself deeper. I tried to wrap my arms around his torso, to pull him into the cab through the open window, longing to feel the strength of his muscles pressed against my skin, but the door was in the way.

Ryan drew away. I leaned back, struggling for breath, my mind racing. *Why has he stopped?*

I hid my disappointment behind anger. "That wasn't fair."

He grinned at me wickedly. "No way, it was *completely* fair. I'm just making certain you have all the facts before you make your choice, Alex."

"What choice?"

Ryan hurried around to the other side and hopped into the seat beside me, nodding to the driver, who pulled out into the street without a word.

Ryan lowered his head toward me and whispered, so the driver couldn't hear, his breath tickling my ear, "I want you to know that I *heard* you, and I respect your needs. You want to be able to choose your mate, to be in control of your destiny. Your parents died and it hurt like hell, and you don't want to fall for someone in case that happens again. You want control, and I get that. You have no idea how much I get that. That's what frightens you about me and what I've told you – you fear your choice has been taken away. Well, I'm giving you back that choice."

"Explain."

"You may take me as yours, or reject me, and I will not force anything upon you. You didn't ask for any of this, and I respect that. But, *I want you,* Alex. That's not just my genes talking." He glanced down, where I could see a bulge through his black jeans. He grinned. "Well, maybe it's my jeans talking."

"Are all artists this bad at puns?"

"Only when we're really trying to impress someone. I've been out of the world a long time, and within 24 hours of meeting you, I'm walking around the village and taking you out to dinner. I think you might be the best thing that's ever happened to me, and I want to be the same for you. I aim to show you what a life with me might be like."

I jammed my hands under my legs, and closed my eyes. His words replayed over and over in my head. *I think you might be the best thing that's ever happened to me ...* That should've scared me, but instead, warmth pooled through my body.

It was so hard to think when Ryan was right there beside me in the car, the scent of his skin mingling with the leather of the seats. I'd only known him for two days – it was far too soon for me to say whether he was ... *my mate.* I tested the phrase under my breath. *My mate.* It was so primal, so protective, so much better than "boyfriend."

It felt almost ... *natural.*

I shook my head. I barely knew the guy. Sure, it felt as if I'd known him for years, because I'd lived and breathed his artwork for so long, but Ryan was not his paintings. He was infinitely more fascinating, more confident, more seductive ...

It's your choice, his words echoed in my mind. He was giving me what I wanted. So, I decided I would give him what he wanted – a chance to win me over.

The cab pulled up to the curb. Ryan grinned at me. "We're here."

He quickly paid the driver, jumped out of the cab and came

around to open the door for me. I stepped out, my head spinning as if I'd already consumed a few glasses of wine.

I was surprised to see we hadn't stopped in front of a restaurant. Instead, we'd parked at a small Tudor cottage at the end of a quiet street bordering Crookshollow Forest. The front path was decorated with fairy lights, and comical witch figurines and ceramic cats peeked up from between the garden rows.

Ryan marched right up to the door, and raised his hand to knock. Before he could, though, the door swung open, and a petite woman of about sixty appeared in the frame. She wore several long black wool shawls and dangly crystal earrings that brushed against her shoulders. Her jet-black hair was pulled back from her face and tied in a loose bun, wisps of it dangling free, framing her kind face and piercing, intelligent eyes.

"Well, well," she drawled, her hand on her chest. "Ryan Raynard, as I live and breathe. You give an old woman a heart attack, calling out of the blue like that, and then arriving three hours late for dinner. I thought I'd be six feet under before I saw you outside the walls of Raynard Hall again."

"I thought so, too." He smiled at her in a tender way. I glanced between them, wondering who she was, and why they seemed to know each other. Why had he brought me here to see a strange old lady?

Ryan stooped down and embraced her, instantly becoming lost in her swathe of black shawls. She patted his back, then pushed him away. "That's enough sentiment from you. I don't want your lady friend to get the wrong idea."

He snorted, and she threw back her head and laughed. She turned to me, picking up my hand and holding it between hers. "You must be Alex," she said. "Come in, come in. Ryan has told me all about you. I'm Clara. I imagine he's told you nothing about me."

"Absolutely nothing at all," I replied, feeling instantly at ease around the woman.

"That is just like him." She laid a hand on my shoulder and led me deeper into the house. It was like no house I'd ever seen before. The walls were nearly completely obscured by all manner of art and ephemera; beautiful impressionist paintings hung next to postcards from Las Vegas dive bars and framed paintings of happy-looking people in strange costumes. I peeked into a cosy-looking living room, and spied a Ryan Raynard original hanging over the inglenook fireplace. Dark, antique furniture was crammed into every corner, every surface bursting with candle stubs, crystals, old leather books yellowed with age, and realistic statues of foxes and wolves leaping and howling.

I leapt back myself as a black cat jumped down from a velvet-covered settee and streaked across the hall.

Clara squeezed my shoulder. "Don't mind Clarence. He's always jumpy around strangers. There was a little boy living next door who used to pull his tail, and he's never quite got over it."

"I hope you gave him a stern word, Clara," said Ryan. "We can't have the young lad thinking that sort of behaviour is okay."

"Oh." She smiled, her eyes dancing. "Don't you worry; I gave him more than a word. Come through here – I've set up for you outside. Alex must be starving." Clara led us out a backdoor. Outside was a wooden porch overlooking a picturesque garden that faded into the dark woods beyond. Fairy lights lined the path to a wooden gazebo entwined in wisteria, beneath which a small table had been set with candles and silverware for two. Champagne chilled in a silver bucket on one side of the table. On the other side, steam poured from beneath a silver dish, warmed with the flame of a small candle placed underneath.

"This is beautiful," I whispered. My stomach rumbled loudly. Clara was right – I *was* starving.

"I thought you'd like it," Ryan replied. He pulled out a seat, and gestured for me to sit. I did so gingerly, not wanting to upset the delicate tablecloth and posy of flowers beside my place.

"Tonight's menu is a watercress salad, followed by *coq au vin* in a red wine reduction," said Clara. "And bitter chocolate torte for dessert. Ryan, do stop fussing and sit down. I'll pour the champagne. Those big, clumsy paws of yours can't be trusted not to spill."

What was going on here? "Wait, Ryan, this isn't right. Clara is your friend. She can't serve us out here like a … like a servant."

"This was her idea." Ryan slid into the chair opposite mine. "I came to Clara because I haven't taken a woman out in a very long time, and she's the closest thing to a woman I know."

"Ryan!"

But his words only made Clara laugh. She cupped her hand on my shoulder and waved my protests away.

"It's my pleasure, dear. In my day, I cooked at the finest kitchens in London, Paris, New York … It does this old heart proud to see Ryan here with a beautiful young thing like yourself."

"Clara, please come sit with us," I begged.

"Nonsense. You two make yourselves at home and I'll fetch the first course." She bustled away, singing under her breath as she disappeared into the house.

I leaned over the table and whispered to Ryan. "Is Clara a shifter, too?"

He shook his head, laughing. "No, and if she were, she'd have such keen hearing she'd be able to listen to you talk about her even when you're whispering. Clara is a witch. She comes from a long line of witches that have had a close tie with Crookshollow for centuries. She's very special to me, as you'll find out, and I don't get to see her nearly enough. Sometimes, when you're used to being alone, even the idea of visiting people who are truly dear to you seems too much."

"You haven't seen her in ages, and you made her slave away in the kitchen, cooking us *coq au vin!*"

"I'll have you know that *I* cooked the food in Clara's kitchen, while she bustled around me, adding two pints of cooking sherry to everything and trying to steal all the chocolate." He raised his glass. "Let us toast."

"What are we toasting?"

"To you, Alex – the beautiful, charming, *infuriating* lady who wandered into my mansion, and my life." Ryan held up his glass. Feeling my face grow hot, I raised my own, touching the glass to his. I would never normally fall for such blatant flattery, but Ryan made it sound both utterly sincere and extremely sexy.

Clara brought out the salads, and we both dug in. As soon as the first leaf was on my tongue, I realised how famished I was. I wolfed down my salad with hardly a word, stopping only to lubricate my mouth with wine. It was *delicious*.

I set down my knife and fork as soon as I was done. Something had been nagging at me. "Ryan if you are happy being a recluse, why did you decide to have an exhibition? Why now?"

He put down his fork, and sighed. "I wondered when you'd ask that."

"It just strikes me as strange, that's all."

"There's more to this story than you know, Alex, but I didn't want to hit you with all of it last night. You might have heard some stories about my father around the village. How he found some witches in the forest, and they cursed him into leaving the manor abandoned while he fled to the Scottish highlands?"

I nodded.

He turned to Clara, who had arrived with the main course. "Meet the witch he found in the forest that night."

Oh. *Oh.*

"It isn't like the stories say," Clara said, as she cleared away my empty bowl, and placed a delicious smelling chicken breast in front of me, piled high with mushrooms and drizzled in a glorious red wine sauce. "We became lovers, but Alistair was consumed by his torn feelings. He came from a long line of vulpines who believed in the importance of keeping the bloodlines pure.

"Men in the Raynard family only mated with other pureblood vixens, ensuring their line continued untainted by ordinary human genes. Taking up with someone like me, who did not have any shifter heritage ... it was an insult to his entire family, and they let him know it. But, he was a man of violent passions, and as much as it tore him up inside, he couldn't stay away from me."

Clara smiled, and she suddenly appeared decades younger – her beauty immobile, made even more luminous by the wisdom of her years. I knew then that theirs had been a great love, for what man could have found her in the forest and not been utterly mesmerised by her?

"We were as careful as we could be, but still, I fell pregnant. Alistair's father told him on no uncertain terms that if I had the child, Alistair would be disinherited. Alistair said he did not care. They were out hunting in the forest, and they got into a bitter fight. His father bit Alistair on the neck, accidentally opening a vein and killing him."

She paused then, her eyes searching the heavens, lost in the memories of her love. I stared at Ryan, watching his expression as this story unfolded. His grandfather had killed his father, over him? What a horrible thing. What had it done to him, growing up knowing that?

And how was Ryan not like the other mutts? He seemed to have complete control over his shifting, and he had Raynard Hall. How had that happened if his genes were all messed up and his grandfather hated him?

Clara wasn't finished. "Without Alistair, I didn't know what to do," she said. "I was young, and pregnant, and very, very afraid. I knew the Raynards would try to kill me before I gave birth to my cub, for they did not want a mutt or a human child to have a claim to Raynard Hall. My parents disowned me when they found out I was pregnant out of wedlock. I had no one to turn to, so I did what any young girl pregnant with a shapeshifter's baby would do – I ran away to London and fell in with a bad crowd."

I laughed. "Of course. That's probably what I would've done."

"I did the best I could, working in kitchens in the city and staying with friends until I could afford my own place. I built a network of people who helped me and who nurtured Ryan's creativity – he spent his childhood hanging out with musicians and artists and other radicals. I taught him to control his shifts, and sometimes I took him to Hyde Park and let him run free." She patted Ryan's hair. "Piece by piece, I built a life for us – it wasn't the life he would have had in Raynard Hall, but it was a life full of colour and unique people.

"Even though I had no contact with the shifter community, I knew Ryan was special." Clara smiled at her son. "He wasn't the kind of mutt Alistair had talked about with such distaste. But then, he wasn't wholly human, either. It seems my own magical lineage might have passed down a unique range of genes, but I don't know for certain. For whatever reason, Ryan has all the powers and abilities of a full-blooded vulpine."

Well, that explained that, then.

"When Ryan hit puberty, his vulpine genes started to work in overdrive. Imagine your typical angry teenage boy, and add a fatherless household and some feral fox genetics, and you have the wild, surly son I did my best to care for. It had become evident to me that Ryan hated the city. He craved the forests, the trees, the rivers. He wanted to roam, and he wanted to hunt. My city life was holding him back."

Clara left then, returning to the kitchen. We both picked at our meals in silence while I digested everything she'd said. I met Ryan's eyes, wanting to ask him all sorts of questions about his father and his life in London, but my words caught in my throat. Finally, I said, "So what happened next?"

"I ran away," he said. "I'm ashamed of it now, but at the time, I felt I had no choice. I packed up my paints and a change of clothes and hitchhiked across the country. Eventually, I ended up in Belfast. There are great tracts of wilderness near the city, where I would retreat for days at a time. I met other shifters there – some friends, some not. I started to learn about this other side of me, the side I had to hide when I lived in London with Clara.

"And the more I learned about the shifter world, the more I craved a territory of my own. In Ireland, I was always an outsider, always a subordinate to the established clans there. Clara wrote to me from London, telling me my grandfather had died recently, and if I wanted to, it would be safe for me to return to Crookshollow. There were no other heirs. Raynard Hall was officially mine."

Clara came out again, and set down a slice of torte on a beautiful china plate in front of each of us. I grabbed her arm as she turned to leave.

"Please stay and enjoy dessert with us," I said. "I want to hear all about your life in Crookshollow."

Ryan pulled over an embroidered ottoman, and Clara begrudgingly sat herself down. Ryan pushed his torte toward her, then got up to go to the kitchen to cut himself a slice.

Clara watched me as I finished off the last of my chicken. "Ryan tells me you're a Fauntelroy," she said.

I nodded, my mouth full of buttery mushrooms. "I didn't know about my connection to the vulpine world until yesterday."

"I knew your mother," she said. "She was a woman of singular kindness and wit. From what Ryan tells me, you've inherited many of her traits. I was so sorry to hear she died."

"Yeah, me too." I swallowed the lump that rose in my throat whenever I thought of them.

"I liked you the moment you walked in my door," Clara said, taking Ryan's champagne glass from the table and draining it in one gulp. "And I'm picky about people. So is he. If Ryan has chosen you, he must think you're truly something special."

"I'm told there's not much choice in the matter, for either of us," I said.

She waved her hand. "Oh, that old 'fated to be together' line? Vulpines have been telling themselves that nonsense for thousands of years. Personally, I don't believe it. Sure, they can sniff out potential mates who have the best chance of giving them pure shifting offspring, but the clans are so in-bred now that it's all just a genetic pic'n'mix, when it comes right down to it. No, the real magic isn't in finding the one you're destined to be with, it's in forging the bond that two people make together that enables them to endure when one of them becomes another creature."

Ryan returned then with a slice of torte for himself, and another bottle of champagne, which he poured into our waiting glasses. I dug into my torte, the delicious chocolate ganache running over my tongue, as I gestured for him to continue his story.

"When I returned to Crookshollow, I tried to convince Clara to move into Raynard Hall with me, but she wasn't having it. She knew me too well – even in that huge house, her presence would be too cloying, too close for me. But she did move back to the village, to be near to me. I spent the first couple of years here repairing some of the damage the decades of neglect had done to my ancestral home."

"You could've fooled me." I thought of the crumbling façade and overgrown gardens.

"It's a huge task, and one that likely won't be finished in my lifetime. I don't like having lots of workers around the place. I didn't paint for four months while they refurbished my own suite of rooms, but it was worth it to get rid of the moose heads and mahogany in one area of the house and create something more conducive to making art. Finally, I could establish my own territory, and work in complete solitude, and I could be close to Clara, to protect her. At night, I roamed the forest, and little by little I fought off the other vulpine clans that had ensconced themselves in the Raynard territory and reclaimed Crookshollow as my own. As the years went by, my life in the forest, and my art, became my driving force, and so I took myself out of the world, becoming more and more like my father, letting my fox side control me. Until you came along."

Ryan paused. He reached across the table and clasped Clara's hand, meeting her eyes. The love that flowed between them was fierce, primal, bound by bonds of blood. He would do anything to protect her. This was a side of Ryan I'd never seen before, the side of him that was utterly human.

"So what has changed now? Why the exhibition?"

"Over the last few months there has been an influx of new shifters into Crookshollow Forest," Ryan said. "Not just foxes, but wolves and birds and badgers and deer and all types of shifters. They're responsible for all those animal maulings and attacks. Most are mutts, like Marcus, but I don't think they're doing this on their own. You mentioned a name last night – Isengrim. That is the name of a powerful lycanthrope, a wolf-shifter."

"A werewolf?"

"Yeah, that's another word for them. They're one of the most ancient and powerful shifter species. Wolves and lycanthropes were once common in Britain, but they became too bold, decimating livestock and desecrating burial sites, digging up the bodies. The species were completely eradicated by the 19th century."

"So why's this guy still around?"

"Isengrim is a rogue lycanthrope. He left his clan in the Black Forest and came to England as a stowaway on a fishing boat a few years ago. He has some dangerous ideas about the place of shifters in the world, and he's been moving up and down the country, gathering followers. He's stirred up other rogues and the whole mutt population with dangerous thoughts, bringing chaos and disorder to the delicate shifter dynamic. He wants shifters to rise up, to not only make themselves known to humans, but to take over control of the country."

I paled. "Is that ... is that a good idea?"

"Some think so, but most do not. At different times

throughout history, shifters have been known to humans. That's why so many different cultures have shapeshifter and skinwalker myths. It's never ended well."

"Define well."

"Usually mass genocide." Ryan's eyes were dark. "Shifter species have been on the brink of extinction several times. The general wisdom is that it's better for our self-preservation to remain secret."

"What do you think?"

He face clouded over. "I think Isengrim isn't the right man to lead shifters to revolution. He's dangerous."

"Okay then. If he's the one behind Marcus' attack, then I'm with you."

"A few weeks ago, I saw Isengrim on the edge of the forest, and ever since, more and more mutts and rogue shifters have entered the forest, dancing dangerously close to my territory. As an old magical area, and an important part of shifter lore, Crook-shollow is an ideal place for Isengrim to launch his attack. The clan who holds this area could theoretically command all the shifters in Britain. And that's what I believe Isengrim plans to do. He has a lot of supporters, even in some of the old, powerful clans and packs – dangerous shifters who want free license to hurt humans, who they believe to be inferior.

"All that's standing in their way is me, and my old territorial claims on the village and the surrounding forest. They can't just kill me – I'm too well known, and I have too many allies to make that a good idea. If other shifters come to stop them before Isengrim has built up his army, their rebellion will be over before it even began. They either have to wait until they're powerful enough to not care, or they have to get me to hand over my rights. But because I have nothing and no one in my life they care about – they have no idea Clara is here – they have no leverage. We're at a stalemate. Edgar and the other ravens have been watching my home for weeks, waiting for a chink in my armour to reveal itself.

Effectively, they have me trapped here – if I leave Crookshollow to search for help, they'd step in and claim my land in my absence, and it would take me time to assemble my allies and take it back, and by then it would be too late. They're hacking my computer, monitoring my phones. I can't get a message out to my allies to come and help. I'm effectively on my own."

"So what do you do?"

"I paint." Ryan grinned. "In my paintings are messages – to the shifter clans I know in Ireland, in Germany, in the Americas. These messages call them here to help me put this unrest down before it turns to bloodshed."

"You had to get your paintings in front of the world, so the shifters could see what was happening in Crookshollow," I breathed.

"Exactly. They all know me. They'll be curious as to why I've chosen now to go public with my work. They will be watching. I just have to hold the fort until they arrive."

"Does Isengrim know about the paintings? Won't he try to stop you?"

"He will suspect. More and more shifters are arriving every day. He's trying to swell his ranks before the exhibition. If he feels he's not ready, or wants to send a message of his own, he may try to sabotage it."

"Shit." My stomach churned. Thousands of people would flock to Crookshollow to see the paintings. If what Ryan said was true, they'd all be in terrible danger.

"But now the situation is even more dire. Because now they know you're here and they can sense my connection to you. Suddenly, they have leverage against me. That's why I have to protect you, and why this exhibition *has* to go ahead, no matter the cost."

"But this doesn't make any sense. If I'm what they need, why did Marcus break into my house to scare me? Why would he not try to kidnap me?"

"If Isengrim kidnaps you, then more than likely you'll end up dead. And Marcus doesn't want that, because then you'd be useless as a mate. More than he is loyal to Isengrim and his fellow mutts, Marcus wants a mate to redeem his bloodline. He'd probably convinced Isengrim that for their first foray into my territory, they would simply try to destroy the paintings and frighten you into cancelling the exhibition."

"It's worked." Panic was beginning to rise up within me once again. "If it's so dangerous, if these shifters are just lying in wait to grab me, why are we sitting out here, where anyone can see us? Why are we eating dinner and touring the art gallery like nothing is wrong?"

Ryan touched my knee, the warmth of his hand calming me. "It's okay. We're well inside my territory, and Clara has powerful protective spells around this place. They wouldn't dare come here, and they won't be able to sense either of us through her barriers. They don't know where we are. The gallery, your flat, in fact the whole town is part of my territory, and they won't attack there in daylight, not until they are ready. It's relatively safe, while you're with me. Do you see now, Alex, that the exhibition *must* go ahead."

I glanced up. The moon had risen high in the sky, tinging the horizon with an ethereal blue glow. I stared into Ryan's eyes and saw the moon reflected there – flecks of blueish light against those deep brown orbs.

"I don't want to stay at my flat tonight," I said, shivering as the cold night air touched my bare arms.

Clara reached across and squeezed my hand. "You've learned so much tonight that you must digest," she said. "Ryan, take Alex back to Raynard Hall. She needs a nice bubble bath, and maybe another glass of wine."

That sounded ... perfect.

Ryan dragged me to my feet, his other hand flying across the keyboard on his phone, texting the driver to come back. I began to walk with him toward the house, casting a last, lingering glance at the beautiful, fairy-lit grotto Clara had created for us.

"Wait!" Clara bent down, and from the folds of her shawl, she pulled a small velvet pouch. She pressed it into my hands. "For protection," she said. "Keep it with you at all times."

I tucked the pouch into the pocket of my jacket, and embraced her. "Thank you," I whispered. Clara was wonderful. I adored her already.

The cab driver took us back to the building across from Halt where my car was parked. Panic seized me as I stepped out of the car. I scanned the car park, hunting for animals hidden in the shadows. My hands shook uncontrollably as I pulled my keys out and went to climb into the driver's seat. Ryan slipped in between me and the door, his eyes ablaze. "I'll drive," he growled.

I was barely holding it together as it was, without having to endure more of his driving. "No, you won't. Don't ruin this beautiful night by being an arse. This is my car, and you drive like a person who hasn't been on the road in ten years, so it's either I drive us back to your place, or you take a long, pleasant walk through the mean Crookshollow streets. And you're meant to be protecting me, remember?"

Ryan shot me a filthy look, but he obeyed, sliding into the passenger seat beside me. I pulled out of the building and eased into the street. The clock blinked the time, 12:14. Traffic had eased off for the night, and people gathered in the outdoor leaners lining the windows of the pub at the far end of the high street. I wound the window down, listening to the sounds of laughter and light conversation floating through the crisp air, straining my voice to hear the flutter of wings or bark of a fox behind me.

As I drove back through the streets toward Holly Avenue, near the edge of the forest, I stole a glance at Ryan. He was staring out the window, his expression unreadable. I wondered what he saw when he looked at me – what did it feel like to find the girl who supposedly was meant to be your destiny? What was it like to discover she didn't feel the same connection?

Or did she?

I wasn't sure. I definitely felt *something* in his presence ... a kind of magnetic pull I couldn't explain away. In the two days I'd known Ryan, I'd seen so many sides of him. The arrogant, rich *artiste,* the protective fox, the sensitive, the lonely painter who cries over a Picasso, and tonight ... he'd been so charming, so sweet, so honest. I wanted so badly to peel away all the layers of him, to see if anything else lay deeper.

I glanced up at the mirror and noticed something odd. A car was following close behind me down a residential street. A bad feeling twisted in my gut. I turned down a side street. The black station wagon behind me turned, too.

We exited the residential street along one of the main industrial roads. Warehouses lined both sides of the street – many abandoned now that Crookshollow was mainly a tourist village. I slammed my foot down on the accelerator, but the car behind matched my speed. I ran through a light just before it flipped to red. The black wagon careened through, narrowly avoiding sideswiping a white lorry.

I was been followed.

14

RYAN

"Alex," I said, concerned. I noticed her fingers were clenching the wheel so tightly, the knuckles had turned white.

"Don't turn around, but that car behind us ... I think it's following us."

"What?" How had I not noticed this? *You're too busy thinking about Alex, that's how.*

"It's turned down the last two streets after us, and it even ran a red light back there in order to stay on our tail."

I pulled down her visor, using the mirror inside to see behind us. Alex turned into Peach Street, heading in the opposite direction to Raynard Hall. The car turned as well.

Shit. She's right.

I focused my mind, calling my vulpine senses close to the surface, straining to hear the voices soaring through my head. I caught a whiff of him, faint, but distinctive. He was nearby, all right.

"I can sense Marcus, and there's someone else ... someone he greatly fears, who he believes to be dangerous." I didn't have to say his name. We were both thinking it.

Isengrim.

"What are we going to do?" Alex's voice rose in pitch. Her eyes were wide and bloodshot.

Think, Ryan. Think. "Turn right up ahead," I said.

She swung the car around, heading up the narrow forest road. There were no houses along this road, and no street lamps, either. Tall oaks zoomed by, thickening as we sped along the edge of Crookshollow Forest. After a mile or so, the trees towered all around us, blocking out the moon. The road became dirt, and Alex's Fiat bounced over the holes. Branches bent low over the road, scraping the roof as we lurched by.

Something pushed our car from behind, jerking us forward. Alex screamed as her hands flew off the wheel. I reached over and grabbed it, keeping the car from spinning off the road.

"Alex, you've got to calm down!"

"They're trying to ram us off the road!"

I whirled around, just in time to see the black wagon slam into us again, nudging us off the edge of the road, just inches from a tree trunk. Alex grabbed the wheel from me and yanked it back, slamming her foot down on the accelerator as hard as she could to gain some distance from our pursuers. We careened through the trees, branches scraping along the doors. I kept my eyes locked on the road, watching for the gap in the trees I knew was coming up.

"I don't want to die in a horrible car crash, all mangled and bashed up," Alex moaned.

"I *told* you to let me drive. Now hold on!" I leaned over and yanked the wheel hard to the left. Alex screamed as the car spun off the road and hurtled down into a ditch.

I'd timed it perfectly. We bounced along at an angle, slipping down the large gap in the trees without hitting anything. I directed the wheel across the bank, but the car shuddered over something and two of the wheels came off the ground. The wheel spun free in my hands.

Shit. This isn't good.

The car rolled forward the bank and hurtled down a steep slope. Trees zoomed past us. Branches flew at the windshield. My stomach flew into my ears.

My body jerked forward, my face slamming into the airbag. We'd hit something. The force echoed through my bones, so that everything disjointed and rattled about. My ears rung, my head rattled into a pulp. Spiderwebs crackled across the windshield. Someone was screaming. It took me a few moments to realise it was Alex.

I have to get to Alex.

Without thinking, I flung my door open and pulled myself out. I sprinted around the car and grabbed the handle of Alex's door and tried to yank it open. It wouldn't budge.

Alex pounded on the glass, screaming. "It won't open!"

I glanced down, and realised why. In the dim light of the moon, I could just make out the tree against the bonnet. It had collapsed into the driver's side of the car, the mangled frame locking her door shut.

I could get her to climb over the seat and go out my door, but she was in a panic and I knew it was only a matter of time before they found us down here. I grabbed the edge of the door, calling up my fox from within. My nails dug into the gap between the door and the car. I sucked in a breath, and yanked hard.

The metal groaned. The door tore away in my hands. I tossed the metal aside, and grabbed Alex, pulling her down against the soft earth. My fox pushed against my skin, the smells of the forest driving him wild. He begged to be released. *Soon. Not yet.* I had to take care of Alex first.

I didn't have time to stop to check she was okay. Behind us, wheels spun on the track, people shouted. Whoever had been following us was coming for us again. I dragged Alex to her feet and pulled her further down the bank, into the forest. I passed the door in a crumpled heap, one side jagged where it had been torn from the body of the car.

I scooped Alex into my arms and tore into the trees. Branches scraped my face and arms as I crashed through the forest. My boots slipped on the damp earth, struggling for traction on the steep ground. Alex's head bounced wildly, and she wrapped her arms around my neck to help keep a hold.

Behind us, branches broke, and a man swore.

"They're not giving up!" Alex cried.

"No, they're not." I dropped to my knees, rolling Alex onto the ground behind a massive oak. I tugged my phone from my pocket and pressed it into her hands. "There's a flashlight app on the dashboard. You need to run to Raynard Hall as fast as you can. We're not far now. Just down at the bottom of this hill, you'll see a stream. Follow it and it will lead you to the edge of the back gardens. When you reach the backdoor, ring the bell three times. Simon will let you in. He knows the signal. Do you still have the protection spell Clara gave you?"

Alex nodded, fingering the pouch in her pocket. "I don't want you to leave me."

"I know, I don't want it either. But I need to take care of these guys, and I want you as far away as possible when I do."

"What are you going to do?"

"Something I've done horribly badly up until now," I growled. "I'm going to protect you."

I stepped away from her, and with one hand, tugged apart the domes that replaced the buttons on my shirt. I yanked it off and shoved it into Alex's hands, then slipped off my boots and tugged off my jeans. She stared at me, her eyes bugged out of her head.

"Stop trying to watch me undress," I growled, moving behind the tree. I tied the laces of the boots together, and threw them over a tree branch, then folded the jeans and pressed them into Alex's hands as well.

"What are you doing?" she hissed. "This is hardly the time."

"I told you, I don't like to waste things. Take those clothes back to the house with you. That's a nice jacket. I don't want it ruined out here."

"What about your boots?"

"I have clothes stashed all over this wood, in case I need them. These boots are waterproof, and they'll come in handy one day. Now, run!"

Alex turned on her heel and ran into the trees, her skirt flapping behind her as she flung herself down the slope. My chest wrenched as she disappeared from view. I hated separating from her, but it was necessary.

I turned toward the rise of the slope, crouched on all fours, and set my fox free.

My skin tugged against my bones, as the bones themselves cracked and split. Pain tore through my chest as my ribs folded back, my spine bending and curling. My organs shuddered in my chest as they rearranged themselves. My knees twisted, the cap shifting as my leg bones bent backward. I dug my fingers into the dirt, gritting my teeth as my jaw mangled itself into a new, long shape.

My vision blurred, the world around me swirling through a maelstrom of grey gloom, before presenting itself anew as a delicate net of scent trails.

A compelling itch spread across my whole body as fur sprouted from my skin. I wanted nothing more than to scratch myself to oblivion, but when I glanced down, my fingers had become short toes, a sharp claw protruding from each one.

My tail swished, the sensation again bizarre. I lifted my nose to the air, and sniffed. They were right up the hill, hurtling down toward me.

Oh no, you don't. The thought coursed through my mind. I didn't care who heard it. They needed to know they couldn't mess with Alex.

I crouched behind the tree, coiling the tension in my body,

ready to spring. On the path above, a twig snapped. I leapt into the air, landing in the dirt in front of a sandy-coloured fox and an enormous, snarling wolf.

Hello, boys, I growled, baring my teeth. *Glad you could drop by.*

I held the phone out in front of me, the dim light illuminating tree trunks as they streamed past my face. My heels kept slipping from my shoes, slapping against the insoles like wet flip-flops. I half-ran, half tumbled down the rest of the bank, landing in a prickly bush at the bottom. I pulled my shaking body upright, and half ran, half stumbled onward into the gloom. Water rushed by on my left.

The stream!

At last, something was going right. I ran alongside, the phone out in front of me, just able to make out the thin stream of water from its glow. From back up on the bank, someone howled in pain. *Ryan? Was that him? Is he okay back there?*

Keep going, Alex. You have to make it to the house. You're no good to Ryan if you're wolf food.

Even holding the cellphone out in front of me, the tiny circle of light only gave me a few feet of visibility. Stones rolled under my feet as I scrambled along the bank, gasping for air. As quickly and silently as I could, I followed the trickle of water as it meandered toward Raynard Hall, and safety.

Something growled from the bushes on my left, on the other

side of the stream. Not daring to look, I poured on speed. My heart pounded against my chest, and my breath came out in short, ragged gasps, but I pushed my body to keep on running. I could hear the creature moving through the trees, smell its fetid breath as it came closer, closer.

Ryan, get your arse back here and help me, I screamed inside my head. *Something is hunting me.*

Another growl, closer this time. It was coming up right behind me. Snarling, teeth gnashing, hot breath on the backs of my legs.

Lights flickered through the trees up ahead – large square lights from the windows of the house. *Nearly there.*

I poured on speed again. My lungs gasped for air.

Just as the dark shapes of the garden beds came into view, my shoe caught on a tree root sticking out of the ground.

I toppled sideways, skidding across the sharp stones of the stream bed. The skin scraped away from my arms and knees.

I came to a stop half in the stream, the cold water stinging my ruined skin. *Where's my attacker? Why hasn't he torn my throat out?*

No time to wonder. I dragged myself out of the water and tried to pull myself to my feet, but something heavy landed on my back, pinning me to the stony ground.

Ah, there it is.

Its breath was hot against the side of my face as its snout nuzzled my ear. I could feel the bristly hair of its snout rubbing against my neck. A foul stench wafted across my nostrils – the smell of blood and rotting meat.

My lungs screamed for air, and my heart thundered against my chest. I tried to wriggle away, but a sharp pain in my shoulder kept me pinned down.

The creature's claws dug deeper into my shoulder, and I cried out. I could feel its hair rubbing against my skin as it pressed closer – close enough to tear my face off in one snap of its powerful jaws. It growled in my ear – a low, powerful rumble that turned my body to jelly.

I closed my eyes. *This is it. This is how I die. At least the bite will be quick—*

I heard a squeal, and the creature was torn from my back. I screamed as its claws slashed my shoulder. I grabbed at the stones beneath me for grip and raised myself up, flinging my head around in time to see a huge shape fly through the air and land in a heap a few feet from where I lay. It wasn't a fox, but a great grey wolf with glowing yellow eyes, its beautiful coat filthy with dirt and mud. It no longer snarled, but whimpered, licking at a nasty wound on its leg.

I whirled back around, and saw Ryan in his fox form standing behind me, his body rigid, his tail swishing with anger as he poised for another attack, his eyes narrowed, ready for the kill. He barked at me. Weirdly, the bark registered in my head as a word, as clear as if the fox had spoken in English.

That word was *run.*

I scrambled to my feet, my aching body screaming in protest, and sprinted toward the lights. Each step jostled my torn shoulder, and as I ran, I sobbed with the pain of the gaping wound. I could feel my own warm blood flowing down my back. I fought through the pain, driving my legs forward, pushing myself to fight for safety.

I cleared the forest, and my feet slapped against damp, dewy grass. I raced down a flagstone path, weaving between ornate statues and elaborate topiary beds. I cleared the steps three at a time, screaming as the pain tore at my shoulder. Behind me, I heard growls and snarls as more creatures emerged from the trees, each one desperate to bring me down.

The door – I was nearly there! I fumbled for the bell, jabbed it three times. I collapsed against the ornate carved panels, banging my fists against it, knowing any moment that something was going to come up behind me and finish me off.

Paws thudded across the cobbles, claws clinking against the concrete path. I couldn't hear anything inside the house. I pounded on the window. "Simon," I cried. "Let me in. Ryan's out here and he's in trouble!"

The door flew open, and I toppled on to the marble floor. Simon stared at me, disbelief written across his face. He went to help me to my feet, but a flash of red darted between us. *Ryan.* His paws skidded on the marble. He yelped as he hit the side of the staircase, and crumpled into a heap.

Outside, something snarled as it raced across the lawn towards us. A dark shape running straight for the door.

"Close it!" I screamed. If that thing got in the house, we'd be doomed.

Simon slammed the door shut, just as the beast crashed into it. I heard wood splintering. It howled as it clawed at the solid door, scratching at it with the same claws that had torn open my shoulder. Simon slid the old-fashioned bolts across, punched a combination into an alarm box, and scattered a handful of herbs from a nearby urn across the threshold.

"The manor is protected," he said to me, though it sounded as if he were trying to convince himself. "They can't get in here without breaking through some powerful magical charms. Nevertheless, we should move to a less exposed part of the house."

I nodded, my head spinning as shock started to set in. My legs buckled beneath me, and I slumped against the door, sliding down until I sat on the cool marble tiles. I watched the fox as if in a trance, unable to quite connect my thoughts together in my fuzzy mind.

Eyes filled with pain, Ryan pulled himself on all fours and moved deeper into the house, dragging his right hind leg behind him. I could see a trail of blood following him across the marble.

Shit. He's hurt. I hoped like hell it wasn't bad.

Spindly, thin hands lifted under my arms, dragging me to my feet. "Quickly now," said Simon, supporting me with his own body as he shuffled down the hall after Ryan. "He's injured, and I need to tend to his wounds. In his fox form, he doesn't like humans to touch him. If he hides too deep in this house, I'll never find him."

I let Simon lead me across the opulent entrance hall. We followed Ryan down a corridor, up a narrow flight of stairs, and down another wide corridor into a brightly painted drawing room – another room, like Ryan's light-soaked gallery, completely stripped of the stuffy, formal English furniture that adorned the rest of the manor. This must be one of Ryan's personal rooms.

Simon laid me on a sofa, then closed and bolted the doors.

"Please," he gestured to the pile of bright cushions beside me. "Make yourself comfortable. There are drinks in that cabinet if you need something to calm your nerves. I'll fetch you food in a moment. I need to attend to him." I heard Ryan's claws clacking against the waxed wooden floor, deeper in the room.

"My shoulder—" I moaned. The pain was becoming unbearable.

Sighing, Simon turned to me, pulling a first aid kit from a drawer beneath the liquor cabinet. He sat on the coffee table, facing me, and quickly cleaned my wounds. He peeled the backing off a dressing, and pressed it onto my shoulder. I tried to turn my head to look, but he pushed my chin gently away.

"It's a nasty cut," he said kindly. "But you will heal."

He then cleaned the scrapes on my knees and palms. When he had finished, he handed me two pills, and a glass of whisky. "For the pain," he said. "I know you shouldn't mix these with alcohol, but I think in this case we can make an exception."

From somewhere behind me, Ryan whimpered. Simon whistled. Ryan gave a short yip in response. I watched, numb with shock and fear, as Simon reached inside a high cupboard and pulled out a towel. He bent down in front of Ryan, who had hidden behind an overstuffed chair on the far side of the room, and lovingly rubbed his fur dry. "Let's take a look at that leg," he said.

Ryan whimpered again, the sound tearing at my insides. "Don't hurt him," I whispered.

Simon shushed the fox. "You know it is much better to dress wounds while you're in fox form, Master Ryan." He pulled the first aid kit across the table and got to work cleaning, stitching, and wrapping Ryan's wound. Ryan sat on the towel, his whole body shaking. He didn't cry out again.

"Excuse the master," Simon said kindly as he dabbed at Ryan's matted fur, while Ryan panted. "If he's exerted himself a great deal, it takes him a few minutes to gain the strength to shift back to human form, especially when he has been injured."

"I understand," I breathed, gulping down the scotch, enjoying the warmth as it circled my throat. "I'm a little tapped of strength myself."

Simon got up, took my empty glass, and poured me another drink. He handed that to me, and then filled another two glasses, raising one to his own lips. "I hope you don't mind scotch. Ryan has his particular tastes, of course, and we don't often have visitors, so I don't have much else on hand."

I only nodded; staring at the fox slumped beside the door, panting as he licked at his wound. My stomach clenched tight. *Oh, Ryan, please be okay.*

The whisky was starting to take effect, warming me from the inside out. The sting in my shoulder subsided into a dull ache. Simon and I sat opposite each other, drinking in silence, watching the fox try to tug off the bandage, waiting for Ryan the human to materialise.

"You can touch him," said Simon kindly. "If you wish."

I set down my drink, and knelt beside Ryan. His breathing was laboured, and he stared at me with large brown eyes filled with pain. I reached out a hand toward him, letting him sniff it, nudging it with his snout.

Please be okay, Ryan. Please don't be dying. I couldn't handle it if you were dying.

He snorted, his warm breath tickling my hand, and I smiled, despite my fear. I leaned down, reached around his neck, and hugged him to me, running my hands through his thick, soft fur, feeling his chest rise and fall with every breath. I buried my head in his fur, taking in the woody scent of him. "Please come back to us, Ryan," I said, feeling my tears fall against him. "I choose you."

Slowly, in my arms, I felt the fox begin to change. Beneath his fur, Ryan's bones were reforming, elongating and twisting to become human limbs. His fur shrank away, revealing warm, clammy flesh. I held tight to him as his body twisted under my touch, and in a few moments, I was holding Ryan the human, *my* Ryan.

He raised his arms and embraced me in return, the heat from his body like a fire inside my heart.

"You are safe," he breathed into my ear. "That's what matters."

I laughed, tears streaking my face. "You had me worried there for a minute, when you wouldn't change back."

"I'm here now," he said, stroking my hair. I rested my head on his shoulder.

"Master?"

I looked up. Simon was standing above us, holding out a warm robe.

Ryan looked up at his butler. "Thank you once again, my friend," he said, his voice unusually tender.

Reluctantly, I moved away from him so he could pull the robe over his muscled shoulders, drawing it closed over his sculpted chest, covering his beautiful body. "My bandage is now a little tight. If you could look at that, and then check the windows and doors, make sure the protections are still in place."

I extracted myself from Ryan's grasp so Simon could re-bandage his leg. I watched as he removed the bandage, my stomach turning as I saw the long gashes splitting the skin.

Simon had neatly stitched them up, but they still looked bad. *Poor Ryan.* My shoulder wound hadn't been bad enough to need stitches.

When Simon was finished, he helped Ryan to his feet, and handed him an ornately carved wooden cane to help him support his leg. "I'll leave you in Ms. Kline's capable hands," he said, then left.

I was alone with Ryan once again.

Ryan grinned at me, his knuckles white as he gripped the cane. "Well, that was some adventure," he said, pulling on the collar of his robe.

"It certainly was."

"You were hurt." He looked so serious. "I was such a fool. I should've known there were two of them, that they would split up."

"Is that what happened?" I showed him the shoulder wound. "I assume that wolf was Isengrim. He's a cheerful character."

"He certainly is."

"Why didn't Clara's protection spell work on him? Why was he able to touch me?"

"He's strong enough to push through it," Ryan said. "Although not strong enough to do any real damage. That wound is pretty shallow."

"It doesn't *feel* shallow." I winced.

"If you hadn't been wearing that charm, he would've eviscerated you right there."

"How delightful. How about you? Are you in an awful lot of pain?"

"I've had worse," he grunted, as he shuffled toward me. "I don't want to talk about it. I don't want to talk *at all*."

He narrowed the space between us in a flash, and once again I found myself lost in those wide, brown eyes. He reached up with his free hand, and grazed my cheek, his fingers dancing over my temple, stroking my forehead, cupping my chin. My breath caught in my throat.

I didn't want him to stop.

Ryan held my chin up and leaned in closer, his lips brushing mine. *Soft, so soft and tender.* Not like the kiss earlier in the evening. Not what I expected from his eyes filled with lust and passion. Gently he prised open my lips, and his tongue entwined with mine. My whole body coursed with warmth, aching for him to touch me, to take me rough and wild.

Ryan reached up with his hands to cup my cheeks, pulling me closer. I leaned against him, pressing my body against his. A moan escaped my lips as he slid one arm across the small of my back, lifting my shirt so he pressed his palm against my skin.

His fingers crept up my spine, reaching up to unclasp my bra.

Yes, yes! I wanted him so badly, wanted to feel the warmth of his fingers all over me. I kissed him more forcefully, my tongue exploring the depths of his mouth, inviting him deeper into mine.

The next thing I knew, his wounded leg buckled beneath him and he fell heavily against me, his teeth knocking against mine as we collapsed in a heap on the floor.

"I guess I can't put as much weight on this leg as I thought." He smiled weakly, wincing as he picked himself up and held out a hand for me. He stared me up and down, no doubt taking in my dishevelled appearance, wild hair, sodden, dirty clothes, and bandaged shoulder. *Is he rethinking his passion?*

"Ryan—" I began.

With a look of determination on his face, he snatched up his cane, and grabbing my hand, dragged me through the drawing room into another long, dark hallway. He kicked a door open, and yanked me inside.

Ryan flicked on the light, and I gasped in awe. We stood in an opulent bedroom decorated in an elaborate, sensual style. Red velvet drapes hung from the curtains, held back with gold ties. In the centre of the room stood a large oak bed covered in red silk sheets and gold damask pillows. Above it, hanging from the ceiling, were two large, gilded mirrors. I felt a shiver of excitement run down my spine as I wondered what it would be like looking up into those mirrors. *Is this where we—*

Ryan hobbled across the room and threw open a wardrobe door, revealing row upon row of women's garments. I followed him into the enormous wardrobe, running my hand down a rack of evening dresses, feeling the sumptuous silks and chiffons slide through my fingers. Another rack held winter coats in an assortment of rich, dark colours. Buttery soft leather jackets hung next to tight black jeans and designer t-shirts. At the back of the wardrobe stood row after row of shoes – sky-high red heels, black motorcycle boots, wedges and flats in every colour of the rainbow.

"This is what you wanted to show me? That you're secretly a cross-dresser?"

"You're lucky you're so beautiful." Ryan grabbed me around the waist and kissed my neck, sending another delicious shiver down my spine. "Your sense of humour could really turn off a man. These are for you, Alex. Your clothes have been ruined. It's the least I can do. Choose what you need for the night."

He thinks I'm beautiful. While choosing fresh clothes was the last thing on my mind, I thought I might be able to find something sexy to wear for him. I turned to the wardrobe and buried my face in the racks, hiding my flushed cheeks amongst the designer garments. In a shelf near the back, I found lingerie – silk negligees, lace teddies, all the typical stuff that wasn't my style at all. In a drawer under the shelf, I found a silk pyjama set that was halfway between prostitute and grandmother. *Perfect.* I also found some jeans and a t-shirt in my size, for the morning.

Why does he have all these women's clothes? I brushed the thought aside. The guy had just saved my life, again. This wasn't the time to be giving him the second degree. I didn't want anything to ruin the moments to come.

Just thinking about that huge bed and those gilded mirrors sent a delicious ache through my whole body.

Ryan gestured to a pile of towels in another alcove, then opened the door to the ensuite. "You'll find everything you need in here," he said. "Just ring the bell by the door if you need something, and Simon will bring it up to you."

I sat down on the corner of the bed, realising that he intended for me to sleep here ... alone.

Disappointment surged through me. "You're leaving me here?"

He stared at me with hard eyes. "It's been a long night, Alex. I am in pain, and so are you. We both need to rest."

"But you're supposed to be protecting me. Where's your room?"

He raised an eyebrow. "That's awfully forward."

"I didn't ... that is ... I mean ... I just want to know you're close by, in case a certain wolf comes back for me."

"He won't be getting inside this house," Ryan growled.

"Ryan, I ..." I squeezed my eyes shut. *I can't believe I'm saying this.* "I don't want to go to sleep, and I certainly don't want to sleep *alone.* I told you, I chose you. What happened?"

In a moment, he crossed the space between us, leaning against the bed, bracing his bad leg on the oak frame as he loomed over me. "I heard you," he growled.

"Then why—"

"I'm trying desperately to be a gentleman here, Alex. All I want to do is rip your clothes off and fuck you senseless. But this would mean I would mark you officially, and all this fate stuff is difficult for you. I get it, and I don't want to frighten you. I'm trying to ..."

My heart skipped. He was so close to me, his face ferocious, wild, and his eyes bored into mine with an intensity I'd never seen before.

"You need to run away, *now,*" he whispered, his words dark, menacing. "You have no idea what you're playing with."

"I'm not running," I whispered back, daring him to give in to that animal nature I knew lurked just below the surface.

Ryan's lips met mine with a force that knocked me backwards. Like fire, his lips scorched mine, his tongue a flame searching for something larger to burn. His hands were everywhere; cupping my cheeks, entwined in my hair, pressed into the small of my back. Ryan shoved me against the silken sheets, crawling on top of me, his kisses forcing my head deeper into the slippery folds. His heaviness made me feel protected, consumed by him.

He kissed a line of fire from my mouth, across my jawline, and down the sensitive skin on my neck. Ryan's hands moved up my arms, his fingers knitting with mine.

I arched my back, pushing my body closer to him, longing to feel that fire inside of me. With one hand still holding mine, he used his other to unhook the buttons on my blouse, his fingers just grazing the bare skin underneath, making me ache for him. I held my breath, watching in the mirror above me as his muscles rippled across his back.

But before he'd even undone all the buttons, Ryan stopped. He lifted his head, and his gaze flicked around the room. He sniffed the air, and something flashed in his eyes. Was it anger, or was it fear?

He leapt from me, yanking himself across the room, as far from me as he could get.

What is going on? What have I done to frighten him?

Ryan stared at the ceiling, his eyes wide. He peered around the corner of the door, his stance aggressive, ready to fight off an intruder.

"What's wrong?" I asked, my heart pounding against my chest. I folded my arms across my chest. *Have I done something wrong?*

Do I smell bad? Is there an intruder in the house? Does he not want to ...?

Ryan grabbed my arms and yanked me up from the bed. He kicked the door open with his foot. "I have a better room for you," he growled, pulling me down the hall. I cringed as the door slammed shut behind us.

"Ryan, what's wrong? Did one of the foxes get inside the manor?"

"No, it's nothing, Alex. I just ... needed to get out of that room." Ryan pushed open a door and flicked on a light, revealing a dimly lit room, large, but not overly so. It was painted in a soft, soothing grey, and contained little furniture – just a large bed and a single nightstand. One entire wall was taken up by a single large window, overlooking one corner of the forest and, just beyond, the flickering lights of Crookshollow.

"This room used to be my father's study," Ryan said. "It was decorated with moose heads and dreary Victorian portraits. I chose it for my own, because of the view over the forest. I had that window lifted in with a helicopter. It's one solid pane of glass, so it was quite some undertaking."

I pulled the small pouch Clara had given me from the pocket of my shirt, and placed it around the doorknob. Then, I stepped right up to the window. It reached to the floor, which met the edge of the roof, so the whole room seemed suspended in midair, as if I might drop away into nothing. I peered down at the sprawling lawn and overgrown flowerbeds surrounding a long pool, the dirty water glimmering a deep blue in the moonlight. Solar lights illuminated the paths nearest the house, and beyond the garden, the forest lay in shadow. Instead of its usual calming presence, the outline of those dark, twisted branches seemed menacing. It was too close, pressing in against me, forcing me into a corner. I didn't like it one bit.

I could see dark shapes moving in the garden. "What's that?" I asked, pointing.

Ryan stood behind me, wrapping his arms around me. He looked down. "Enemies," he replied. "Isengrim and his cronies. Marcus is there, too, behind the hydrangea bed."

I squinted in the poor light, and could just make out the back of the sandy-coloured fox. My stomach churned with fear. I could see at least eight large animals down there, stalking the garden, preventing us from leaving. "Where is Isengrim?"

Ryan pointed at a large shape standing on the water fountain. The creature looked up at the moon and I realised it wasn't a fox like the others, but that giant grey wolf with the cold yellow eyes. He stared up at us through the window, his wide mouth pulled back into a snarl, revealing sharp, deadly teeth. "He's the one who attacked you, and tore up my leg."

I shuddered to think I'd been so close to those snapping jaws. The wound in my shoulder ached anew.

We watched the wolf circle the fountain, and then sit on the edge, throwing his head back and howling. The sound reached us, even through the thick glass, and it chilled me inside and out.

Ryan kissed my neck. "Relax, Alex. They can't get us in here."

I pulled away from him. "You can't do this to me."

"Do what?"

"Before, you were ... and then, suddenly, you're prowling around like something is going to attack you." I folded my arms across the chest, keeping my eyes glued on the shadowy forest so that I didn't have to look at him, so that he couldn't see the tears pooling in my eyes. When I spoke, my voice was hard. "What's wrong with me? I told you I wanted to be your mate. So why do you push me away?"

He grabbed my arm and spun me around. "Something startled me," he whispered, his eyes boring into mine. His robe had come undone, revealing the outline of his naked chest beneath it. "The thread of a memory. I am sorry."

"That's not it. It seems as if you're holding back. I see all the wild desire in your eyes, and yet, when you kissed me before, it was tame."

"I'm trying to be gentle," he said. His grip on my arm tightened, the pain sending a shiver of desire through me.

I knew that was what he was trying to do, but I wanted him to stop. I didn't want to sleep with Ryan the sensitive artist; I wanted Ryan the wild, powerful fox man. I wanted the raw, primal lust I saw in his eyes, for that same desire burned below my skin.

"Ryan, you can't pretend to be something you're not. If I am to be ... your *mate*, then you must treat me like one. I want all of you, or I want nothing."

His eyes flickered. "Alex, you don't know what you're asking. The relationship between a fox and his mate is very ... complex. It's an exchange of power, of vital, elemental magic. I wanted to ease you into it. I wanted to give you pleasure you'd never known, but I didn't want to scare you."

"You can't scare me, Ryan Raynard," I said, staring back at him with the fiercest expression I could muster. "Just you try."

As I delivered this, I yanked my arm away. But Ryan was too quick. He stepped in and grabbed my hips, pressing his naked chest against my back, so I could feel the warmth of him through the thin layer of my shirt, feel his hardness pressing against my ass cheeks. I was just where I wanted to be, completely under his power.

This is more like it.

Ryan's hands roamed down my body, his fingers laying trails of fire across my skin. He grabbed the corners of my shirt and yanked it hard. Buttons flew in all directions. I shrugged the sleeves off my shoulders, the ruined fabric slipping to a pile at my feet. Ryan's hands cupped my breasts, as he kissed along my neck, across my jawline. I tipped my head back, and our lips met again.

We devoured each other, our kisses wild and frantic. Ryan walked forwards, toward the bed. When my knees butted up against the edge, he shoved my shoulders down. His hands gripped my shoulder and shoved me down, so that I sat on the edge of the bed.

Ryan picked up my ankles and lifted my legs over his shoulders. Before I had a moment to think, he thrust his head between my legs, his tongue licking the whole length of me, sending a shiver of delight through my body.

I fell back on the bed, watching his red hair bob in front of me as his tongue searched out every inch of me, lavishing attention upon my throbbing clitoris. The ache in my body intensified, and my stomach tightened as my desire grew hot and insistent within me.

Ryan tilted his head back, so his eyes met mine, dark with passion. His tongue danced over me, sending me closer and closer to the edge.

The ache exploded into a wave of pleasure. The orgasm tore through me, more intense than any I'd ever had before. My back arched, lifting off the bed, and for a brief moment, I lost myself as stars danced across my vision.

Ryan stood in front of me, and shrugged off his robe, revealing his powerful, muscled body in all of its naked glory. His shaft stood erect – the skin pulled back to reveal the engorged head, primed and ready for action. It was by far the largest I'd ever seen, an almost terrifying length that seemed far too large to fit anywhere in my body. As I stared at him, I felt an ache pressing against my core, a strong, primal desire to take him into me, every glorious inch of him.

I dropped to my knees on the floor, and wrapped my arms around his legs. *Fair's fair, right?* I wanted to give him as much pleasure as he'd just given me. A low moan escaped his throat as I rubbed my lips against the tip of his enormous shaft. I opened my mouth, and took him, slowly, slowly, an inch at a time. His tip brushed the back of my throat. But still, I could not fit the whole length of him inside my mouth. I lifted myself up on my knees, lowering myself back down and moving him in and out of my mouth. He tasted warm, and slightly salty.

Ryan moaned louder, his fingers gripping my uninjured shoulder. I sucked him faster, swirling my tongue around his tip. I loved the way my mouth felt stretched around his shaft, tasting his saltiness on my tongue. He moaned as I worked him, digging his nails into my shoulder, and I could feel his whole body begin to tense. Just as I thought he was about to burst, he grabbed me under the shoulders and hauled me onto the bed.

Rolling me onto my stomach, Ryan pushed my naked body against the sheets and climbed on top of me, pinning me with his weight. He shoved his knees into mine, forcing my legs apart.

Yes, yes!

My whole body ached with need of him. I hadn't been with a man in so, so long, and I didn't remember it feeling this good. I wanted him so bad.

Ryan's nails scraped down my back, leaving tingling trails across my skin. He jammed his hand between my legs, his fingers finding that little spot from which all my aching came. He pulled and rubbed it roughly, and the ache grew within me again, beginning to creep out through my body, threatening to overwhelm me. Unable to move at all, I gave myself over completely to him, moaning as his touch moved me closer and closer to orgasm.

"Don't move," he growled in my ear. "This will hurt."

I didn't care. I was too far gone. I couldn't have moved even if I wanted to.

Ryan moved his lips to my neck, and as his fingers continued to work me, he bit down against me, pulling my head back against him. I cried out as his teeth broke my skin, and searing pain rocked through my body. While he bit deeper, he continued to rub his fingers around that little bud. The pain fought against the growing pleasure spreading through my lower body, each sensation fighting for dominion.

The pain won, sweeping through my body in a great wave of

agony. It felt as though a cool liquid trickled through my limbs, turning my whole body cold – except for the mound between my legs, which burned with a blazing fire. I could feel a strange energy flowing from Ryan's mouth into my body – a shimmering magic transferring into my veins through the coldness. I tried to cry out, but my lips were numb, my breath frozen in my throat.

My body grew colder. My veins turned to ice, the cold seeping into my lungs and pricking at my skin. It was as though a thousand tiny needles pierced my skin at once. The pain in my limbs became unbearable. I screamed silently as Ryan's bite held me paralysed. He rubbed my clit faster and faster, until the ache inside burst forth, the searing heat boiling over, pressing back against that painful cold. Tongues of fire burned through my body, washing away the freezing pain and bringing my body back from the brink.

Both the fire and the ice abated, leaving me weak and wounded. Ryan let go of my neck, dropping my head against the bed. I gasped for breath, my entire body shivering with a strange sensation, a kind of tingling numbness.

"Now I have claimed you," Ryan whispered in my ear. "We are bonded together."

Oh. So that's what that was. My body relaxed as the heat of my orgasm abated. If this was us bonded together, then *bring it on*.

Ryan flipped me over, so that I faced him once again. My hands were pinned beneath me, forcing my back to curve upward at an awkward angle and my breasts to jut out. My eyes landed on his, and there I read the hunger of a hunter spying a deer in the distance. He bent over my chest, scraping his teeth across my nipples, enjoying the shudder that ran through my body.

I tried to wriggled my hands out, longing to reach up and touch him – to run my fingers over his wide, muscled chest. But he placed a hand around my wrist. "Close your eyes, Alex. This is for you. Focus on the feelings, the sensation. Trust me, it's even better."

"Okay." I kept my hands behind my back, my fingers digging into the sheet as Ryan's tongue swirled around my nipples. All my hairs stood on end and delicious shivers ran through my body. The black metal boyfriend had been into blindfolds and hogties, so I was no stranger to the joy of abandoning my senses to heighten pleasure. And if what was to come was anything like what he'd already done to me ... well, bring on the blindfolds.

As if he was reading my mind, Ryan threw the corner of the duvet over my head, so I lost sight of him. I fought against the folds of the fabric, but this only made him clamp the sheet down tighter. "Don't fight," he warned me, a delicious glee in his voice. "I'm not going to hurt you ... much."

His words filled me with a delicious terror. I don't know what he'd done to me, but it made every inch of my body shimmer with a kind of magical ecstasy. Ryan moved between my legs, and I felt something warm slide over my wet folds, dancing over the spot that gave me such joy. *His tongue.* I ached for him, longing to feel his hardness inside of me.

Not being able to see him made the experience even more erotic. He licked and sucked, reaching up with his fingers to twist my nipples, first softly, but then harder, so hard that my chest soon ached with pain. The strange energy he'd transferred to me took that pain and spread it through my entire body, pressing it against the fiery pleasure that once again threatened to overwhelm me. My stomach swelled with the pressure building inside of me, tendrils of pleasure reaching out through my arms, down my legs, across my chest, filling my body with warmth.

Ryan scraped his nails across my inner thigh as he buried his head between my legs, his tongue darting into every fold of my most intimate place. I felt his stubble along my thighs, his long hair tickling my sensitive skin as his tongue worked its magic. The pressure in my stomach burst and the warmth flooded me. I cried out as the orgasm carried me away, my vision disintegrating into a thousand red splodges – like one of Matisse's decoupages coming to life before my eyes – and my limbs kicked and jerked of their own accord.

Before I had even recovered, Ryan climbed on top of me, pinning my legs with his. I heard him tear open a condom and roll that on, and then he thrust deep inside me. I cried out as his length filled me, pressing against my wetness on all sides. Frantic and wild, he came at me with abandon, thrusting with such force and ferocity that the bed around us creaked in protest. The sheet still covered my face, and I could see nothing but flashes of silk and bright red spots.

But I could *feel* everything, more powerfully than I ever had before – every stroke, every touch, every thrust. The energy in my body flared up once more, only now it seemed to be swirling all around us, enclosing us in a cocoon of shimmering, sizzling magic. Feeling him move inside of me while he swirled his fingers around my tight nipples made the pressure bubble up inside of me once again, starting between my legs and rising like steam through my belly and chest.

Ryan tore away the sheet from my face, and covered my mouth with his, his tongue darting possessively into every corner and crevice. We rocked against each other. I could no longer tell where his body ended and mine began. Ryan's fingers closed around my breasts, squeezing them, pushing them together, making them ache and throb. The pain and pressure built inside of me, and became one in my body, crawling through my limbs and reaching right down to my toes. I cried out as another orgasm rippled through me, my moans muffled by Ryan's forceful tongue. Fire coursed through my limbs, and I bucked against him as I fought to gain control over my body. All the while, the strange magical energy danced over my skin.

Heedless to my passion, Ryan continued to pound against me, his thighs slapping against mine. He twisted my nipple hard, and a moan escaped my throat as the last of the fire within me faded into a dull, warm ache. I bucked against him, rising up to meet each stroke. We began to move together, slamming against each other with enough force to knock the bed against the wall.

Finally, Ryan's own orgasm claimed him. He cried out and collapsed against me, his whole body clenching tight, then releasing. When he had completely emptied himself, he rolled me over and pulled the sheets around us both, wrapping his arms around me and holding me against his warm body. The air around us seemed alive, crackling with residual energy.

"You are mine, Alex Kline," Ryan whispered into my ear. "And I am yours."

16

ALEX

A noise woke me. The creak of a door opening.

I opened one eye, then the other. The room was unfamiliar. Where there should've been a pile of clothing and walls covered with bright prints and a calico cat sprawled across the bed, there was only light streaming from a large picture window overlooking the forest, soft grey walls and a warm figure snoring beside me. It took me a few moments to remember where I was.

What a night.

The memory of the sex – the incredible, mind-blowing, world-moving sex – coursed through me. I rolled over, rubbing my eyes to rid them of sleep. There was Ryan, his muscular arms curled around his pillow, one hand reaching lazily across the bed toward me. His chest moved up and down slowly, and he emitted an unattractive, wheezing snore. He was still asleep. Behind him, I saw the door to the room creak open slowly.

I reached behind me and pulled my phone from the dresser. The time read 7:29. "Is that you, Simon?" I called, wondering if Ryan's dutiful servant was bringing us breakfast in bed. *I could get used to this lifestyle.*

No reply. The door creaked open a little more.

I pulled at the laces on the front of my pyjama top, trying to stuff my breasts back inside. "I'm not sure we're exactly decent at this moment."

"Nothing is ever decent in this room," a sultry voice replied.

I looked up again. A woman stood at the doorway, wearing a red silk gown with a plunging neckline that clung to every inch of her perfect body. Tawny red curls fell over her shapely shoulders, framing a porcelain, heart-shaped face and emerald eyes that sparkled with all kinds of wanton promises. She was the most beautiful woman I'd ever seen, which was odd, because something about her also seemed familiar, as though I'd seen her before. But I'd definitely remember a woman like that, wouldn't I?

As I watched – too shocked to cry out – the woman lifted the small pouch from the doorknob, raised it to her bow-shaped lips, and sniffed delicately. Screwing up her face in disgust, she tossed the protective spell into the hall.

"Wake up, sleepyhead," she cooed at Ryan's sleeping form, stepping into the room, her red gown swishing around her shapely legs.

I realised with a jolt where I recognised her. She was the woman in Ryan's paintings. She was the Fox Woman.

That's not possible. Ryan said the Fox Woman didn't exist. He said she was just a symbol. How can she be here?

"Who are you? How did you get in? The house is locked up and protected by magic."

She narrowed her emerald eyes at me. "Who are *you*? What are you doing in this room?"

"I'm Alex Kline. I'm his ..." I glanced over at Ryan, his face still. I kicked him with my foot, hoping to wake him up. But all he did was snort, and continue sleeping. What was I to him? I didn't know how to articulate it. The word *mate* still wouldn't fall off my tongue. "... I'm his art curator. Who are you?"

"I'm surprised he hasn't mentioned me," she smirked, tugging at the ruby choker around her thin, elegant neck. "My name is Melissa St. Clair. I am Ryan's mate."

TO BE CONTINUED

∾

Want to find out what happens next? Check out book 2 of the Crookshollow Gothic Romance series, *Art of the Hunt* - READ NOW

∾

Want free books, exclusive giveaways and exclusive sneak peeks at upcoming Steffanie Holmes paranormal romance books? Sign up for the mailing list to get the scoop.

ART OF THE HUNT

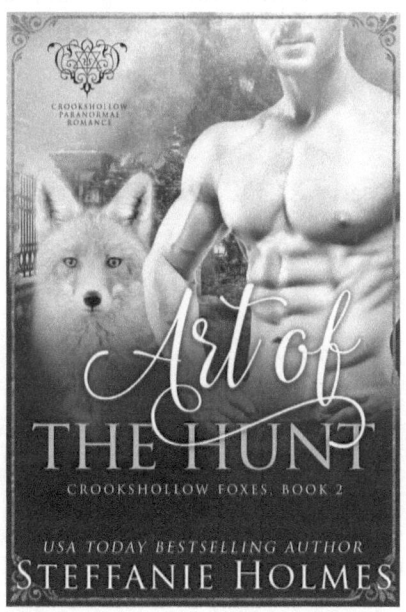

Want to find out what happens next? Grab your copy of Book 2 in the Crookshollow Gothic Romance series

The evil wolf Isengrim has Raynard Hall surrounded, and he's moving in for the kill. Billionaire artist and fox-shifter Ryan

Raynard must protect his mate – the clever curator Alexandra Kline – at all costs. But that's difficult to do when she refuses even to talk to him.

After discovering Ryan's lie, Alex flees Raynard Hall and aligns herself with Marcus, a vicious mutt with his own agenda. But without Ryan's protection, Alex is vulnerable. Isengrim's shifter army are gaining power, and too late Alex realises just how dangerous the enemy really is.

With less than two weeks until Ryan's exhibition launch, can Alex and Ryan find a way to reconcile and stop an army of rogue shifters from killing every last human in Crookshollow?

Reader Warning: *Art of the Hunt* is the second book in the Crookshollow Gothic Romance series by Steffanie Holmes. This book contains scorching sex, adult language, and a cliffhanger ending. If you like dirty, raunchy sex with a hot fox and one clever, sarcastic heroine, then this book will have you howling for more. Enjoy!

Read ART OF THE HUNT now

EXCERPT FROM ART OF THE HUNT

"Holy shit." Kylie had her hand over her mouth.

We were standing at the top of the bank, looking down at my car. Or rather, what was left of my car.

Deep ruts in the dirt marked the spot where Ryan and I had left the road and hurtled down the bank. The front right side of the car had plowed into the tree, folding upward like an origami crane, the metal bent and twisted. One wheel lay in the dead leaves a few feet from the wreck, the tire torn to shreds. Seeing it in the daylight, my stomach churned with fear.

I couldn't believe I'd survived that.

My mind flashed back to the last time I'd seen a crash site: the police incident photos from my parents' accident. The grisly images were plastered all over the local newspapers – mangled steel, torn tires, scorch marks across churned-up earth.

No. I jammed my fists into my eyes. *You can't think about them now. Focus on the present. What do you need to do now?*

Taking a deep breath, I started walking down the hill. "Alex!" called Kylie. "What are you doing? What if it's dangerous? What if the engine explodes?"

"This isn't a Guy Ritchie film," I yelled back. "I'm looking for my purse."

"Don't leave me here with him," Kylie pouted, walking a little closer to the edge of the bank to watch me. Marcus sniggered. "He's naked and strange."

"If you fall and break your neck, princess, I'm not coming after you," Marcus yelled. He still sat in Kylie's car, using a torn strip from his t-shirt to mop up the blood from a claw mark on his leg.

Ignoring them both, I half-walked, half-slid down the slope, each step jolting my wounded shoulder. My bare feet crunched over dead leaves and dry sticks. Up close, the car was even worse than I'd realised. I slid past the driver's side door, which lay in the leaves several feet from the car, a great dent in the middle of it. Jagged metal teeth curled up from one side, where it had been torn from the car.

Ryan. He'd torn that door away to rescue me. I hadn't really thought about it much last night, after all that had happened. Now I marvelled at the strength he must possess in order to do that. Perhaps being a *vulpine* gave him more strength than an ordinary human, as well as super hearing.

But that doesn't stop him being a liar, I thought angrily. I swiped at my eyes, trying to force away the tears I didn't want to cry. Ryan wasn't worth the tears.

I blinked, and my gaze fell on a pair of boots hanging in a branch not far from the car. Ryan's boots.

Don't think about him now. He chose to lie to you. It's over.

I stepped closer, and peered inside the car. I had been driving, so I would've placed my purse on the backseat. I pulled open the backdoor on the passenger side, and searched through the empty takeout containers and dirty laundry. Where was it? I leaned over and felt under the seats.

Nothing. It wasn't there.

As I stood up, I noticed something on the back of the driver's seat. It was a paw print, caked in dirt. I rubbed the edge of it. Dry.

It was from last night.

I backed away from the vehicle, my mind spinning. My purse was gone, and shifters had been in the car. They had taken it. Which meant they had the keys to our flat. They had a swipe card for the Halt Institute. They had my mobile phone and date planner, with contact details for all my colleagues and friends.

Holy shit.

TO BE CONTINUED ...
Read Art of the Hunt now

WANT MORE STORIES FROM THE WORLD OF CROOKSHOLLOW

Haven't read the Wolves of Crookshollow series yet?

Sink your teeth into the hot werewolf paranormal romance from *USA Today* bestselling author, Steffanie Holmes.

Now FREE on all platforms!

Anna

It's been five months since my boyfriend was tragically killed in a climbing accident. I didn't think I was over him ... until Luke walked on to the archaeological site.

Tall, dark, sexy, tattooed, funny, dangerous. Everything I want in a man.

But he's hiding something. He acts strangely in the moon-light. He won't tell me anything about his life. And I caught him trying to destroy an important find.

My body aches for him, but my heart tells me I'm not ready to make myself vulnerable again, especially not for a guy who isn't being straight with me.

If only ...

Luke

Anna Sinclair – archaeologist, geek girl, totally and utterly delectable.

I knew from the moment her intoxicating scent wafted across my wolf senses, she's meant to be mine.

And that knowledge is *terrifying*.

The last thing I expected was to find my fated mate on an archaeological site. Whenever I'm near her, all I want to do is claim her.

But she's broken. The last thing she needs in her life is a werewolf out for revenge. I'm here to destroy the site, to keep my family's past buried forever.

If Anna finds out the truth, she'd never speak to me again.

But I can't deny the bond between us. **I'll do anything to make her mine.**

Digging the Wolf is a standalone paranormal romance by USA Today bestselling author Steffanie Holmes. Read if you love archaeological mysteries, badass wolves, a broken heroine, and a hero so hot he'll have you howling for more.

OTHER BOOKS BY STEFFANIE HOLMES

This list is in recommended reading order, although each couple's story
can be enjoyed as a standalone.

Nevermore Bookshop Mysteries

A Dead and Stormy Night

Of Mice and Murder

Pride and Premeditation

Memoirs of a Garrotter (available May 2019)

Briarwood Witches series

The Castle of Earth and Embers

The Castle of Fire and Fable

The Castle of Water and Woe

The Castle of Wind and Whispers

The Castle of Spirit and Sorrow

Crookshollow Gothic Romance series

Art of Cunning (Alex & Ryan) - READ NOW FOR FREE

Art of the Hunt (Alex & Ryan)

Art of Temptation (Alex & Ryan)

The Man in Black (Elinor & Eric)

Watcher (Belinda & Cole)

Reaper (Belinda & Cole)

Wolves of Crookshollow series

Digging the Wolf (Anna & Luke)

Writing the Wolf (Rosa & Caleb)

Inking the Wolf (Bianca & Robbie)

Wedding the Wolf (Willow & Irvine)

Fallen Sorcery Fae (shared world)

Hollow

Witches of the Woods

Witch Hunter

Coven

The Curse (coming in 2018)

Want to be informed when the next Steffanie Holmes paranormal romance story goes live? Sign up for the VIP Readers Club at https://www.subscribepage.com/briarwoodprequel *to get the scoop, and score a free bonus epilogue to enjoy!*

ABOUT THE AUTHOR

Steffanie Holmes is a USA Today bestselling author of steamy historical and paranormal erotic romance. Her books feature clever, witty heroines, wild shifters, cunning witches and alpha males who get what they want.

Before becoming a writer, Steffanie worked as an archaeologist and museum curator. She loves to explore historical settings and ancient conceptions of love and possession. From Dark Age Europe to crumbling gothic estates, Steffanie is fascinated with how love can blossom between the most unlikely characters.

Steffanie lives in New Zealand with her husband and a horde of cantankerous cats.

Steffanie Holmes Mailing List

Want free books, exclusive giveaways and exclusive sneak peeks at upcoming Steffanie Holmes paranormal romance books? Sign up for the mailing list to get the scoop.

Join the conversation! Learn more about Steffanie:
steffanieholmes.com

www.ingramcontent.com/pod-product-compliance
Lightning Source LLC
Chambersburg PA
CBHW020618120726
47905CB00003B/842